PRAISE FOR THE EROTI
EDITED BY J. H. BLAIR

The Good Parts

"If you ever flipped through a book looking for the juicy stuff, *The Good Parts* belongs on your nightstand. Fifty contemporary American writers . . . break taboos, quicken the pulse, and make you sweat. All in one sex-filled volume." —*Playboy*

"Have fun." —*Detour* magazine

"A quality collection of beautifully written pieces that happen to be about sex . . . fascinating and revealing." —*Publishers Weekly*

"This is a quick, fun read." —*Library Journal*

The Hot Spots

"A broad, less strictly sexual definition of erotic defines this anthology. Its selections are nothing if not diverse, with vignettes that capture love among adulterers (Bliss Broyard), librarians (Aimee Bender), cybersluts (Martha Baer), hustlers (Scott Heim), and hookers (Laura Kasischke)." —*Entertainment Weekly*

¡Caliente!

THE BEST EROTIC WRITING IN LATIN AMERICAN FICTION

edited by

J. H. BLAIR

BERKLEY BOOKS, NEW YORK

A Berkley Book
Published by The Berkley Publishing Group
A division of Penguin Putnam Inc.
375 Hudson Street
New York, New York 10014

This book is an original publication of The Berkley Publishing Group.

Collection copyright © 2002 by The Reference Works.
"Introduction" copyright © 2002 by J. H. Blair.
A complete listing of individual copyrights and acknowledgments appears on page 201.
Cover design by Erika Fusari.
Cover photograph by Alvin Booth.
Text design by Tiffany Kukec.

PRINTING HISTORY
Berkley trade paperback edition / June 2002

Visit our website at
www.penguinputnam.com

Library of Congress Cataloging-in-Publication Data

Caliente! : the best erotic writing in Latin American fiction / edited by J. H. Blair.
        p.   cm.
   Includes bibliographical references.
   ISBN 0-425-18466-8
      1. Erotic stories, Latin American—Translations into English.   2. Latin American
fiction—20th century—Translations into English.   I. Blair, J. H.

PQ7087.E5 C25 2002
863'.6080358—dc21

2002019538

PRINTED IN THE UNITED STATES OF AMERICA

10   9   8   7   6   5   4   3   2   1

⊰❙ CONTENTS ❙⊱

v

Contents

Contents

◄[Introduction]►

IN THE UNUSUALLY HOT NEW YORK JULY OF 1993, MY FRIEND KATE told me she'd found a perfect novel for the heat wave the city was then enduring. The book was Christina García's *Dreaming in Cuban*, which I read over a three-day (100°F, 102°F, and 99°F) stretch. In addition to its many other virtues (intelligence, passion, exultant lyricism, generosity of spirit, etc.) the book, a poignant saga of three generations of Cuban women, was filled with food. Food in Cuba:

> *His mother serves him huge portions of chicken and rice, filling his plate twice. Ivanito eats three of the warm plantains in brown sugar syrup and drinks mango juice chilled with ice.*

> *At home his mother removes her tunic and slippers. She takes a hammer and rusty chisel and shatters each coconut, scraping the blinding white, perfumed flesh from the shells. Ivanito helps her blend the coconut with egg yolks, vanilla, condensed milk, sugar, cornstarch and salt, and hold the empty tin vegetable-oil containers while she fills them with the mixture. Together they arrange them in the freezer. With the leftover egg whites, she fashions star-shaped meringues, which she serves with the ice-cream day after day, for breakfast, lunch and dinner.*

And food and New York:

> *On Fifth Avenue, Lourdes stops to buy hot dogs (with mustard, relish, sauerkraut, fried onions, and ketchup), two chocolate cream sodas, a potato knish, lamb shishkabobs with more onions, a soft pretzel, and a cup of San Marino cherry ice. Lourdes eats, eats, eats like a Hindu Goddess with eight arms, eats, eats, eats, as if famine were imminent. The refrigerator cakes come in flimsy cardboard boxes steaming with dry ice. There are Grand Marnier cakes and Napoleons with striped icing and Chantilly cream. Lourdes unpacks three Sacher tortes and a Saint Honore' studded with profiteroles, Linzer bars with raspberry jam, éclairs, and marzipan cookies in neon pink. In the summer, there'll be fresh peach strudel and blueberry tarts. In the fall, pumpkin pies and frosted cupcakes with toothpick turkeys.*

I followed Christina García with Francisco Goldman, and Mario Vargas Llosa. By mid-August, and some dozen novels later, I was firmly convinced that regardless of a wide range of fictional styles, it was safe to say this: No one does food, nature, music, or sex better than Latins.

I know, this is supposed to be an erotic anthology not a culinary anthology. But more than their European, North American, African, or Asian counterparts, for Latin/South American fiction writers, the pleasures of reading are the pleasures of the body and the questions they raise are answered with instincts of survival—not the *if* questions but *hows*. The food is rich and the sex is hot. So it follows that the richly sensuous depictions of an exotic array of eatables cannot be separated from the erotic. Faint, simmering undertones of passionate fury hidden under dense layers of overliterate deceit don't stay under for long. Or (to bring in another culture dominated by heat) there's an old Sicilian saying, "Never trust a lover who's not passionate about food."

A few examples. First, from one of the twentieth century's greatest novelists, Gabriel García Márquez:

> *She sampled an Alicante sausage that tasted of licorice, and she bought two for Saturday's breakfast, as well as some slices of cod and a jar of red currants in aguardiente. In the spice shop she crushed leaves of sage and oregano in the palms of her hands for the pure pleasure of smelling them, and bought a handful of cloves, another of star anise, and one each of ginger root and juniper, and she walked away with tears of laughter in her eyes because the smell of the cayenne pepper made her sneeze so much.*

This is vintage García Márquez. Strictly speaking, it's not a sexual description. But we certainly know a lot about the woman's erotic nature by her gestures and her choices, most especially by her crushing the spice leaves in her hands — they're not there for the pleasure of ownership but for their scent; perhaps the most sensual of properties. The latter passage is, of course, list making, but it's truly inspired, highly sensual list making. The ending — the outstretched hand and bulging wineskin — is the quintessential picaresque with implications of hearty, robust, roguish sexuality.

Carlos Fuentes gives us restaurants of the rich and lists that range through home cooking that's been made wildly exotic:

> *. . . the Focolare, the Rivoli, and the Estoril, along with the restaurant that was everyone's favorite, the Bellinghausen, with its* maguey *worms, its noodle soups, its* escamoles *and* chemita

steaks, its delicious flans flavored with rompope *eggnog and its stems of beer, colder than anywhere else.*

By contrast, Laura Restrepo and Louie García Robinson take us outside to give us street markets in all of their atmosphere of a public view of the intense joys of food.

. . . the air begins to fill with a cloud smelling of armpits and fried pork rinds, strolling vendors offer peanuts, puff pastries, oatmeal in pots, slices of pineapple, and ice cones with colored syrups. Eager greengrocers set up tables with blenders to make guayaba, sapote, *and* guanabana *juices. A dubious doctor promotes Iguana eggs in spring water to improve lovemaking. . . .*

. . . much more subtle, but as persuasive, are the smells; the delicious aromas of earn itas, *chicken in* mole *sauce, cooked tongue and other fillings that will go into burritos, enchiladas and tamales in countless District restaurants and taquerias. These aromas, which sweep across* La Michon, *blend with the smell of corn mash in lye that will be flattened and stamped into tortillas and the bouquet of chili peppers of every variety.*

Even though the market is filled with intimate bodies, it's still interesting to note that after the peanuts, pastries, and pineapples, Restrepo, saving the best, most telling detail for last, ends with iguana eggs in spring water for improved lovemaking. Robinson takes the smells of La Michon and makes sure to notice how they mix and rise, leaving the narrator implicit but sensing the effect of the food more than she knows it.

And finally, Jaime Manrique gives us fruit and fish that come in seasonally in amounts that grow thick and thin.

There were times of the year when all they had to eat was whatever fruit was in season: ciruelas, or guavas or mangos *plus black coffee, if they were lucky. Food was plentiful only during the months when the Magdalena produced its annual harvest of fish. Then they had* bocachicos, lebranches, lisa, coroncoros, sardines and bagres, *a catfish that grows the size of a big dolphin.*

Next, a sampling. Excerpts from different writers, from different countries, illustrating different ways to write erotica.

First, from the United States, a personal favorite of mine, Oscar Hijuelos:

She undid his trousers and gripped his big thing with her long, slender hand, and soon she was unrolling a heavy rubber prophylactic over it. She liked him, liked it, liked his manliness and his arrogance and the way he threw her around on the bed, turning her on her stomach and onto her back, hung her off the side of the bed, pumping her so wildly she felt as if she was being attacked by a beast of the forest. He licked the mole on her breast that she thought ugly with the tip of his tongue and called it beautiful. Then he pumped her so much he tore up the rubber and kept going even when he knew the rubber was torn; he kept going because it felt so good and she screamed, and felt as if she was breaking into pieces, and, boom, he has his orgasm and went floating through a wall-less room filled with flitting black nightingales.

This passage isn't the first time I've chosen a little something special from Oscar Hijuelos; he showed up in my first collection, *The Good Parts*, and as long as folks keep reading it, I'll keep finding a place for him. As far as this piece, it's classic stuff. In about 150 words he gives us a totally joyous, robust, wild fuck. And he still surprises us at the end. After all the wild pumping and screaming and hanging from the side of the bed, he closes with the sensation of floating in air accompanied by gentle songbirds. Anyway, all Americans love Keats.

Here's a totally different approach from Cuba's José Lezama Lima.

Farraluque felt like a dazzled horse being bitten at the root by a newborn tiger. His two previous sexual encounters had been primitive; now he was entering the realm of subtlety and diabolic specialization. The second requirement of the sacred Hindu text, in which she showed special proficiency, was in whirling the carpet of the tongue around the cupola of the casque, and then with rhythmic nodding movements carpeting up and down the length of the organ. But with each movement of the carpeting, the woman was cautiously stretching it toward the copper circle, exaggerating her ecstasy, as if carried away by the bacchanal from Tannhauser and directing the frenzy imperiously toward the sinister grotto. When she thought the coordinated nibbling and polishing were about to reach an ejaculative finale, she started to pull it toward the deep shell, but at that instant Farraluque with a speed that comes only out of ecstasy, raised his right hand to the to the madonna's hair, pulled upward with fury and exposed the excited gorgon, dripping with the sweat extracted from the depths of her action.

Lezama Lima is writing here as the (over)educated, mock professorial, grandiloquent, worldly Latinate storyteller. From his full bag of tale-spinning tricks he gives us animal comparisons, references to both myth and opera, purposefully Baroque wordplay ("cupola of the casque") mock-heroic exaggeration ("directing the frenzy imperiously toward the sinister grotto"), and plenty of the real, i.e., "nibbling and polishing" and "dripping with sweat."

Why is it that so many writers feel the need to use the mock professional scholar tone anyway? Is the divide between the passionate and the literate so stark as to require justification that will only get its (deserved) mocking tone later in a piece? This is hardly an issue native to Latin writers. Everyone (myself included) does it, but who's to blame for this stylized squeamishness?

The next excerpt is from Argentina's Mempo Giardinelli. You'll not find a "cupola of the casque" nor a "sacred Hindu text" and no *Tannhauser*. This is straight-up noir.

She reached out her hand, turned off the car lights and turned off the ignition; and she started purring like a cat in heat:

"Do it to me, my love, do it to me," and frantically she opened the zipper on his pants and grasped his sex with her hand, while fumbling desperately with the other to raise her jean skirt. And in the faint moonlight that entered the car, Ramiro again saw the sheen of down on her bronzed legs and the tiny white panties which covered her soft feathery pubic hairs; he knew that he couldn't resist, that he had become a puppet. He uttered some profanities when she, in her arousal, bit his sex, and then he grabbed her by the hair and lifted her up bringing her up to his face, and he began to kiss her. He was furious and bursting, recognizing again the beast into which he had been transformed; and

he moved back a bit in the seat and got on top of the girl, who was straddling him, and pulled off her panties with one jerk. He penetrated her violently, and that moment she let out a scream and began to cry, brutalized with pleasure and desire. They rocked their hips awkwardly, embracing each other, pounding each other on the shoulders to incite the other more; and the whole car was shaking. They continued until they reached a frenzied, animal-like orgasm.

A late-night car-fuck in a car seat with only faint moonlight to illumine the illicit lovers. As in most noir, the protagonist "couldn't resist," and like the act he describes, Giardinelli's writing is "furious and bursting." She initiates, and he can't resist; she bites him, and he grabs her by the hair; then they "rock each other" and "pound each other on the shoulders," the balance and the transformation — it's just such a hot scene.

And now for something completely different.

Abuela Gabriela was a beautiful woman, but beauty was unfortunately her nemesis. There was very little to do in the mountains, and Abuela had a hard time keeping Abuelo's mind off his favorite pastime. He loved guava shells with goat cheese, and Abuela would prepare them for him almost every day. When she boiled the guavas, the aroma would fill the whole house and waft in and out through the windows. Abuelo could smell it before he got off his horse. The moment he climbed the stairs, he would start peeling off his clothes and chase Abuela through the house until they were up in his bed. Abuela Gabriela's skin was a delicate guava pink, and when they made love he nibbled playfully at her breasts.

This is Rosario Ferré of Puerto Rico. (With food again!) Her voice, that of the gentle, lyrical, highly civilized, intelligent woman is the accompaniment to the perfect reflection of her scene of guava shells, goat cheese, and a playful chase that ends in some endearing breast nibbling.

When's the last time you read a really well-written erotic passage about ears? The next excerpt (which features more nibbling) is the elegant, knowing, worldly (and affectionate) voice of Mexico's Francisco Rebolledo.

Perhaps it was that detail that awakened her desire. As she progressed in her amorous apprenticeship, Dona Teresa had gradually grown fonder and fonder of ears. She delighted in nibbling them; her teeth gave her the sensation of something soft and fragile but at the same time resistant and flexible. They greatly resembled — perhaps that was why she liked them — a phallus that has already emerged from its lethargy but has not yet attained the hardness it reaches when it is fully excited. A penis in that state fascinated her; she could spend whole hours at a time playing with it — something that, usually, was very difficult, for naturally, it became excited when it was fondled. Ears, on the other hand, remain in that state the entire time.

For all their abundance, most fetish pieces aren't gentle; they are not exactly made to be, with obsession at their center. Rebolledo transforms fetish detail into a playful (but still very personal) desire.

The final excerpt is from Irene González Frei. To paraphrase Cabrera Infante, she is the only Italian author who writes in Spanish.

We experimented with all different kinds of orgasms: extended and brief, slow and fast; interminable storms and sudden gusts, long detours and rapid shortcuts; the serene progression of someone climbing a mountain and the frenetic ascent of someone caught underwater. With a tongue gently resting upon the subtle equilibrium of a clitoris, through the tenuous lips of the vagina, in them, on the edges and in the intimate recesses of the anus, against the breasts; with the tip of the index finger against the upper, internal wall of the vagina, and the entire finger, or two, or three traveling around any part at all of our burning bodies, inside, outside, near, above, below, all around them. I swear sometimes we came just from looking at each other. All we had to do was want it. And we did it on the bus, on line to pay our bills, in the movies, standing in front of the statues in the Campidoglio, in bed, in the kitchen, in the shower, interrupting sleep or dinner to respond to the call of our passion. Everything made us crave each other.

We had discovered that, more than anything, love is a state of lucidity, perception, the inclination — sometimes intentional, sometimes involuntary — discovering pleasure in all the folds of existence, a third eye; an intuition and a certainty, a new sensibility, and the only one capable of perceiving absolute happiness.

After her laundry list of the hows and wheres of orgasm and all of the new sex like kids, González Frei totally switches gears. She tells us that "love is a state of lucidity . . . the inclination — sometimes intentional, sometimes involuntary," and "of discovering pleasure in all the folds of existence." This lucidity is "the only one capable of perceiving absolute happiness."

Enjoy the collection.

—J. H. Blair

◁ ALEX ABELLA ▷

The Killing of the Saints

As a journalist, a TV news producer, a foreign language instructor (this man is fluent in five languages), a screenplay writer, and a court interpreter, Alex Abella has more than enough to do when he's not working late into the night on tough suspense novels like The Killing of the Saints, *a novel that starts "In Los Angeles, cold weather is like death—it catches people by surprise, leaving them yearning for the warmth of the past," which impresses me as a line that could only come from the best of the slumming angels. This excerpt is from that novel.*

FOR SEVERAL DAYS LUCINDA HAD BEEN GAUGING ME FOR SIGNS OF the spell she thought I was under. Not that she was less affectionate. If anything, her concern increased over my affliction so that she practically overflowed with tenderness, bringing me café con leche in bed, arranging cut flowers throughout the apartment, leaving little notes hidden in the folds of my clothes telling me how much she loved me.

She always took pride in being a cunning lover and at that time she felt compelled to give me greater proof of her virtuosity. She found an inexhaustible supply of things to do with my cock and my mouth so that, after a warm bath and a cold shower, where we would scrub and finger-fuck each other, we'd rush to the bed, teasing and playing with every membrane, every orifice and follicle, joining body parts that no manual I knew had ever conceived of joining, experimenting in ways I had only shamefully fantasized before. I never knew my big toe and second toe would fit so easily into her dripping cunt or that a common everyday vegetable inserted up her ass, while I fucked her from the front, would cause such squeals of joy. I bound her and punished her with my leather belts, whipping her ass until it burned to the touch then sticking my cock in her mouth so that she, tied up to the bedposts and with her eyes covered by a blue silk scarf, would know only pain and penetration as her sensual contact and she would suck my dick like a babe a mother's tit, till I would be on the verge of coming, then I would stick it up her ass until I could delay it no longer then I would whip it out again and explode all over her beautiful blindfolded face, her pink tongue dashing to and fro, trying mightily to catch the white jism that oozed down.

At other times I would be her slave, compelled by strikes of flyswatter or clothes brush to run my tongue up and down every inch of her body, from her black-and-gold-flecked toenails to the roots of her henna-tinted hair; then she would slap me and pummel me till I would cry and then would push me down to the hollow between her legs, holding my head down with both her hands, guiding my tongue, like a darting hummingbird's, to the exact spot in her groove, I spreading open the labia so that her hard little clit would push its way out of the curly bush, demanding to be stroked and pinched and kissed and nibbled. Lucinda would wrap her legs around me, arch her body forward and press even harder, her pelvic bone a fist in my mouth, as she rubbed my lips raw and she would come in torrents of dense, briny juice four, five, six times in quick succession. She then would kick me away, my breath forced out of me and I'd go tumbling to the floor, only to crawl back next to her and ask for her forgiveness as she lay burning, eyes rolled white to all-seeing heaven above.

◁ ISABEL ALLENDE ▷

The Infinite Plan

Isabel Allende is the author of the widely acclaimed international best-seller, The House of the Spirits, *which has been translated into over forty languages. The excerpt is from* The Infinite Plan, *which is, I think, a stranger, more ambitious novel. Born in Chile, Isabel Allende currently lives in California.*

THREE DAYS LATER CARMEN MORALES APPEARED AT THE DOOR OF Galupi's gallery in Rome; she had come directly from the airport, and her suitcases were waiting in the taxi. She was praying that she would find him in, and for once her prayers had the hoped-for result. When she walked in, Leo Galupi, who was wearing a wrinkled linen shirt and slacks and no socks, was discussing the details of the next catalog with a young man whose clothes were as unironed as his. Among the Indian tapestries, Chinese ivories, wood carvings from Nepal, porcelains and bronzes from Japan, and a plenitude of exotic art, Carmen, with her swirling gypsy skirts and faint tinkling of antique silver jewelry, seemed part of the exhibition. When Galupi saw her, the catalog fell from his hands and he stood looking at her as if seeing an oft-invoked ghost. Carmen's thought was that, as she had feared, her unwonted swain had not recognized her.

"I'm Tamar. . . . Do you remember me?" and she walked toward him hesitantly.

"How could I forget!" Galupi took her hand and shook it for several seconds, until he realized the absurdity of such a welcome and took her in his arms.

"I came to ask if you want to marry me," Carmen blurted in a nearly inaudible voice, because this was not how she had planned to do it, and even as she spoke she was silently cursing herself for having blown her chances with her first words.

"I don't know," was all Galupi could think to say, once he could speak, and they stood staring at each other in wonder, as the young man of the catalog disappeared without a sound.

"Are you in l-love with anyone?" she stammered, feeling more and more idiotic but unable to remember the strategy she had planned down to the last detail.

"I don't think so; not right now."

"Are you gay?"

"No."

"Can we get a cup of coffee? I'm a little tired; it was a long trip . . ."

Leo Galupi led her outside, where the radiant summer sun and the sounds of people and traffic brought them back to the present. In the gallery, time had dissolved to Saigon, where they were again in the Chinese-empress room Galupi had prepared for her and where he often stood to watch through a chink in the screen as she lay sleeping. When they said goodbye, Galupi had felt the sting of loneliness for the first time in all his world travels, but he did not like to admit it and had cured himself with stubborn indifference, immersing himself in the rush of business and travel.

With time, he lost the temptation to write her and grew used to the bittersweet emotion he felt when he thought of her. Her memory served as protection against the spur of other loves, a kind of insurance against romantic entanglements. When he was very young, Galupi had decided not to tie himself to anything or anyone; he was not a family man, nor one for long commitments, but thought of himself as a loner incapable of enduring the tedium of routine or the demands of life with another individual. More than once, he escaped from an overly intense relationship by explaining to his indignant sweetheart that he could not love her because in his destiny there was room only for love of a woman named Tamar. That alibi, often repeated, became a kind of tragic truth. He had not examined his deepest feelings because he enjoyed his freedom and Tamar was merely a useful ghost he called on when he needed to escape from an uncomfortable affair. And then, just when he felt he was safe from surprises of the heart, she showed up to collect on the lies he had told other women for years. He could not believe she had walked into his shop a half hour earlier and before speaking another word asked him to marry her. Now she was beside him, and he hadn't the courage to look at her, although he felt her eyes openly scrutinizing him.

"Forgive me, Leo, I don't mean to drive you into a corner; this isn't how I planned it."

"How did you plan it?"

"I meant to seduce you; I even bought a black lace nightgown."

"You don't have to go to that much trouble." Galupi laughed. "I'll take you home so you can bathe and take a nap. You must be bushed. Then we can talk."

"Perfect; that will give you a little time to think," Carmen sighed, with no attempt at irony.

Galupi lived in an old villa that had been divided into several apartments. His flat had only one window toward the street; all the rest overlooked a small, untended garden where water sang in a fountain and vines climbed around ruined statues stained by the green patina of time. Much later, sitting on the terrace sipping a glass of white wine, admiring the garden under the light of a full moon and breathing the perfume of wild jasmine, they bared their souls to each other. They both had had countless affairs and romances; they had traveled in circles, practicing nearly all the games of deception that cause lovers to lose their way. It was refreshing to talk about themselves and their feelings with brutal honesty, with no ulterior motives or tactical considerations. They recounted the broad outlines of their lives, stated what they wanted of the future, and ascertained that the alchemy that had first attracted them to each other was still there, needing only a little goodwill to be revived.

"I hadn't thought about getting married until a couple of weeks ago, Leo."

"And why did you think of me?"

"Because I never forgot you; I like you, and I think that years ago you liked me a little too. Of all the men I've known, there are only two I would want to have with me when I'm sad."

"Who is the other?"

"Gregory Reeves, but he isn't ready for real love, and I don't have time to wait for him."

"What do you mean, 'real' love?"

"Total love; none of this halfway stuff. I'm looking for a partner who will love me very much, be faithful to me, not lie, respect my work, and make me laugh. That's asking a lot, I know, but I offer more or less the same, and for good measure, I'm ready to live wherever you want, as long as you accept my son and my mother and I can travel when I need. I'm healthy, I support myself, and I'm never depressed."

"That sounds like a contract."

"It is. Do you have children?"

"Not that I know, but I have an Italian mother. That will be a problem; she never likes the women I introduce her to."

"I don't know how to cook, and I'm fairly straightforward in bed, but in my house they say I'm pleasant to live with, probably because they don't see much of me — I spend hours on end in my workshop. I'm not much bother.

"On the other hand, I'm not very easy."

"Could you make an effort, do you think?"

They kissed for the first time, tentatively, then with curiosity, and soon with the passion stored up in years of warding off the need for love with casual liaisons. Leo Galupi led this imponderable woman to his bedroom: a high ceiling adorned with fresco nymphs, a large bed, and antique tapestry cushions. Carmen's head was swimming; she did not know whether she was giddy from the long flight or the wine, but she did not intend to find out. She abandoned herself to her languor, lacking the will to impress Leo Galupi with either her black lace nightgown or her skills learned with previous lovers. She was attracted by his healthy male smell, a clean odor without a trace of artificial fragrance, slightly pungent, like bread or wood, and she buried her nose where his neck joined his shoulder, sniffing like a hunting dog on the scent. Aromas persisted in her memory longer than any other recollection, and at that moment the image of a night in Saigon came to her mind, a night when they were so close she had registered his aura, never knowing it would stay with her all those years. She began to unbutton his shirt, but fumbled with the tiny buttonholes and impatiently asked him to do it for her. She heard the music of strings from somewhere far away, carrying the millenary sensuality of India to that room in Rome bathed in moonlight and the light fragrance of jasmine from the garden. For years she had made love with virile younger men; now her fingertips were caressing a back that was slightly stooped and stroking the fine hair at a receding hairline. She felt a gratifying tenderness for this older man and for an instant tried to imagine what roads and what women he had known, but immediately succumbed to the pleasure of loving him, leaving her mind blank. She felt his hands removing her blouse, her full skirt, her sandals, pausing, hesitantly, when he came to her bracelets. She never took them off, they were her final armor, but she thought the moment had come to be completely naked, and she sat on the edge of the bed and pulled them off one by one. They fell noiselessly upon the rug. With exploring kisses and knowing hands, Leo Galupi began to familiarize himself with her body; his tongue moistened her still firm nipples, the shell of her ears, her inner thighs, where her skin shivered at the touch; she felt the air growing dense and panted from the effort of breathing; a glowing urgency flowed through her loins, and she ground her hips and moaned as she escaped him, until she could not wait any longer, turned him onto his back, and swung astride him like an inspired Amazon, clasping him between her knees amid a storm of pillows.

Impatience or fatigue made her clumsy; she twisted and slithered like a snake, seeking, reaching, but she was wet with pleasure and summer's sweat and finally collapsed on him, laughing, crushing him with the gift of her breasts, enveloping him in a rain of unruly hair, and whispering instructions in Spanish he could not understand. They lay like that, embraced, laughing, kissing, and murmuring foolish words in a sonorous mixture of languages, until desire became too great, and at one moment in their playful tumbling Leo Galupi took the lead, without haste, steady, pausing at each station along the way to wait for her and lead her to the farthest garden, where he left her to explore alone until she felt herself slipping into a shadowy void, and a joyous explosion shook her body. Then it was his turn, as she caressed him, grateful for that absolute and effortless orgasm. Finally they slept, curled in a tangle of legs and arms. In the days to come they discovered they had fun together, that both slept on the same side, that neither smoked, that they liked the same books, films, and food and voted for the same party, that sports bored them, and that they regularly traveled to exotic places.

"I don't know how good I'd be as a husband, Tamar," Leo Galupi apologized one evening in a trattoria on the Via Veneto. "I have to have freedom to move around. I'm a vagabond."

"That's one thing I like about you; I'm the same way. But we're at an age when we could use a little calm."

"The thought frightens me."

"Love takes its time. You don't have to answer me right away — we can wait till tomorrow." She laughed.

"It's nothing personal; if ever I decide to marry, you'd be the one, I promise."

"Well, that's something anyway.

"Why wouldn't it be better to be lovers?"

"It isn't the same. I'm too old for adventures. I want a long-term commitment, I want to sleep every night beside my life companion. Do you think I came halfway around the world to ask you to be my lover? It will be great to grow old, hand in hand, you'll see," Carmen replied with finality.

"Good God almighty!" exclaimed Galupi, quite openly pale.

◈ JULIA ALVAREZ ◈

In the Name of Salomé

Julia Alvarez is the author of three novels: How the Garcia Girls
Lost Their Accents, In the Time of the Butterflies *(a National Book
Award Finalist), and* ¡Yo! *She has also published three volumes
of poetry as well as* Something to Declare, *a collection of essays.
This piece is taken from one of her finest works and one that
received hardly enough attention,* In the Name of Salomé. *She
divides her time between Vermont and the Dominican Republic.*

SHE DOESN'T KNOW WHAT TO SAY WHEN HE OPENS THE DOOR, SUR-
prise followed by pleasure dawning in his eyes. She forgets that
these moments between a man and a woman have their own en-
coded meanings and he will assume he knows what she wants,
showing up at his doorstep at eight o'clock in the evening.

But she does not know what she wants, not as he takes off her
suit jacket for the second time today, or fixes her a mojito such as
she has never had before. He is right. She rarely drinks—afraid in
fact, that she might like such numbing escapes too much. She is
watching herself as she tells him about her meeting with her
brother Max, as be brushes back the hair fallen from her chignon
and then without warning pulls the hairpin that releases the dark,
curly mass down her back.

His mouth closes on hers, large and wet and frighteningly alive. She stiffens and pushes him away.

"W-w-what?" He is looking straight at her. He has always been able to read the state of her soul from the muscles on her face, a necessary skill for a sculptor he has told her. But she does not want him to see the cloud of doubt that is descending upon her. She buries her face in his shoulder and lets him stand her up touching the whole length of her body. She is revolted by his big hands, his hardness pressing against her thigh. The word become flesh is not always an appealing creature.

"Are you sure you w-w-want this?" he is whispering in her ear. It could be Max asking her about her march tomorrow.

"Yes," she says as he begins unbuttoning the back buttons of her blouse, slipping his hands underneath, "but not here." Over his shoulder she can see the car from this afternoon parked again at the curb, the brief flicker of a cigarette being tossed by the driver on the lawn. Cuba is closing down. Batista's boys have taken over. It is madness to think that her Lyceum ladies can march down on the docks and change anything, madness to be here with this man when every time he touches her she cringes. But she has already broken free from the old life and there is no going back to it. In the studio they walk through on their way to the back room, she catches a glimpse of the bust he has left uncovered. Her own face stares back at her, fierce and almost finished.

◁| JORGE AMADO |▷

Dona Flor and Her Two Husbands

Born in Brazil in 1912, Jorge Amado has been called a "Twentieth-Century Charles Dickens" and Mario Vargas Llosa feels he is "one of the very greatest of living writers." He may also be Latin America's most widely read writer, having been translated into over fifty languages. The following is from Dona Flor and Her Two Husbands, *perhaps his most popular book.*

THE DOCTOR EMERGED FROM THE BATHROOM IN A PAIR OF CLEAN pajamas, giving off the scent of soap. He was of agreeable appearance; his smile was sincere, his eyes were honest. Vadinho had his hand on Dona Flor's dark rose. Oh, Dona Flor, how can you have sunk so low?

"Teodoro, my dear, you will forgive me, but I don't feel well tonight. Let's leave it until tomorrow if you have no objections."

Not well? The doctor was disturbed. She had already complained that afternoon. Would it be nothing but a simple indisposition? Where were the thermometer, the syrup, the box of medicines? "I don't need anything, my dear, don't you worry. You go to sleep and tomorrow I will be well, completely well . . ."

". . . and at your command," she vowed to herself.

How could she suddenly become like that, so unfeeling, so shameless, so indecent, so lacking in pride? Dona Flor asked herself, feeling a pleasant tenderness for her worried husband and a certain satisfaction in the farce she was playing: she kissed his cheek. But Dr. Teodoro was not satisfied. She ought to take a tablet, some drops, at least a sedative to get a good night's sleep and wake up calm and refreshed. He went to get the medicine and a glass of water. No sooner had he gone than Dona Flor felt Vadinho embracing her.

"You must be crazy. Let go of me! He's coming right back."

Vadinho remarked thoughtfully and impartially: "He's not a bad fellow, this second husband of yours. Quite the contrary. Would you believe, my sweet, that I like him better every time I see him. Between the two of us, you are well cared for. He, for troubles and problems; me, for screwing . . ."

The doctor came with a pitcher of cool water, two glasses, and a little flask of colorless liquid. "Tincture of valerian, twenty drops in half a glass of water, and you will sleep soundly and rest, my dear."

He picked up the dropper and carefully and calmly added the sedative to the water. Did somebody change the glasses while the doctor turned his back for a moment? Who? Vadinho or Dona Flor? But, if that was the case, how was it the doctor, being the competent druggist he was, did not recognize the taste of the valerian? Did a miracle occur? If it did, at this stage of the game, one miracle more or less doesn't impress us, causes us no surprise. Maybe there wasn't even a miracle, and Dona Flor just didn't take the sedative, and the doctor's deep sleep was the consequence of the patter of the rain on the roof and his easy conscience. He barely had time to kiss his wife.

"He's growing horns," Vadinho said, using the fitting term. "Now it's our turn, babe."

"Not here," Dona Flor begged, expending the last remains of shame and respect for her second husband. "Let's go into the living-room."

In the living-room the doors of heaven opened wide, and a song of rejoicing burst forth. "Who ever heard of screwing in a night-gown?" Dona Flor as naked as he, each undressing and completing himself in the nudity of the other. A fiery lance ran through her. For the second time Vadinho had made off with her honor, the first when she was a virgin, now that she was married (and had there been other opportunities he would have taken advantage of them). Off they went through the meadows of the night to the edge of dawn.

Never had they found such pleasure in one another: so free, so fiery, so gluttonous, so delirious. Ah, Vadinho, if you felt hunger and thirst, what about me, on that limited bland diet, without salt or sugar, the chaste wife of a respectful, restrained husband? What do I care about what people think of me? What do I give for my honor as a married woman? Take all this in your burning mouth, which tastes of raw onion, burn in your fire my innate decency, rend with your spurs my former modesty: I am your bitch, your mare, your whore.

They came and went, and hardly were they back when they were off again, going and returning. So much longing and so many goals to achieve, all won, all repeated.

Insolent and beloved, foul and beautiful, Vadinho's voice was in her ear, saying so many indecent things, recalling the joys of other days. "Do you remember the first time I touched you? The Carnival groups were coming through the square, and you leaned up against me . . ."

"It was you who put your arm around me and ran your hand down me . . ."

He ran his hand down her and recognized her: "You have the tail of a siren, your belly is the color of copper, your breasts of avocado. You have put on weight, Flor, you are more filled out, you are delicious from your head to your feet. Let me tell you, I have picked a lot of cherries in my life, a good crop, but there is no cunt that can compare with yours, it is the best of all, I swear that to you, my Flor."

"What does it taste of?" Dona Flor asked, shameless and cynical.

"Of honey and pepper and ginger."

He talked and Dona Flor dissolved in sighs. Vadinho, crazier, more overbearing than ever, fire and breeze. Vadinho, don't go away, never again. If you should leave, I would die of sorrow. Not even if I beg or plead with you, don't go away; even if I command and order you to, don't leave me.

I know I will only be happy if you are not here, if you go away. I realize that with you there can be no happiness, only dishonor and suffering. But without you, however happy I might be, I do not know how to live, I cannot live, oh, never leave me.

Zia Summer

Rudolfo Anaya is Professor Emeritus of English at the University of New Mexico. He has won numerous awards, including the Premio Quinto Sol National Chicano Literary Award and the PEN Center West Award for fiction. This is from Zia Summer, his first book to feature Phoenix private investigator Sonny Baca. You'll probably find it classified under Mystery, but it's much more than that and may just be the best book about the contemporary American Southwest.

"I'LL GET READY," SHE SAID, KISSING HIM WARMLY, HER MOIST LIPS and the look in her eyes promising a night of love. "Don't take too long," she whispered, and disappeared toward the bedroom. They had promised each other that come hell or high water, tonight was theirs. And with the rain filling the house with fresh air and drumming on the flat roof, it couldn't have been better orchestrated.

Sonny smiled as he ran the hot water over the dishes. Then the thought crossed his mind that he still wasn't okay. Maybe he should smoke some grass. Like the spiked wine Tamara had given him. He wouldn't have had a problem then!

He finished the dishes and left them to dry in the rack beside the sink. He was feeling an urgency, and he didn't want to screw it up. It was going to be okay, he didn't need to smoke. He walked into the bedroom where Rita waited. She had put fresh sheets on his bed, showered, and slipped on one of his T-shirts.

"Got any mota?" he asked, surprising himself and her.

"No," she answered. "Do you want some?"

"No, just thought—"

He paused by the open window. Damn! Why had he asked?

"¿Qué piensas?"

"Enjoying the breeze," he said, stripping off his shirt. "The rain."

He looked out the window and enjoyed the coolness of the rain, the soft breeze of night stirring. Lord, it seemed like ages when they had last felt rain, heard thunder, smelled the fragrance of the hot earth as it gave up its rich aroma to the rain.

Rita came and stood beside him, wrapping her arms around him. They stood together, enjoying the warmth of their bodies leaning against each other. The sweet fragrance of rain and wet earth enveloped them. There was nothing like that smell in the high arid plateau. The desert earth was like a woman suddenly opened by the voluptuous caress of the lover. The rain and the earth mixed and rose within the thin veil of mist-cooled night.

The people of the valley understood and responded to the forces of nature that suddenly filled them with passion. Wide sky, clouds, rain, earth, lightning and its sound, the smells released were the essence of passion.

Across the way Don Eliseo's cornfield was soaking up the moisture, the leaves of the cornstalks cupping the precious rain. Don Eliseo had watered the young plants with acequia water all summer, but there was no substitute for rain, the old man always said.

The tall cumulus clouds of summer were feminine, woman-clouds, deities bearing the life-giving rain.

Soft, penetrating rain. Lluvia de amor. All night it would make a soft sound on the flat roofs of the valley. Each rain had a name. Manga de lluvia, falling dark and straight down like a sleeve. Or una manguita, a small sleeve. Lluvia de los corderos, the cold, spring rain of lambing season. In summer the monsoon that came to relieve the dry summer, and which sometimes turned into the "pinche rain" because it ruined cut alfalfa in the field, or a picnic, or a baseball game.

In July the tempestas de lluvia, lluvias fuertes, the thunderstorms of the summer, which came quickly and dumped everything in a few minutes. Those were the quickies of the high desert, the sudden rains that came with booming thunder and caused the floods. To make love during a thundershower was to make quick, hurried love. To be like lightning penetrating the earth.

In September showers moved in as sure as the state fair came around, and so people joked and called it state fair rain. There was a rain for every season, because rain was sacred, life-giving. Now, this first rain was one of those unusual rains for the Río Grande plateau, covering the entire state with a steady drizzle. The gentle mood of rain impregnating the earth was like the semen oozing softly into the juicy darkness of a woman. A rain like this made the rhythm of love slower, long lasting, satisfying. The man's urges and his sperm changed as the seasons changed; the woman's needs and moistness also changed. The ozone of the lightning heightened the urge. The tumbling sound of the thunder that rumbled across the valley with a thunderstorm was the drumbeat of love, or lust.

Everything changed according to the weather; desire came and went according to the storms moving across the wide valley. The rain or lack of rain affected the way a woman cried out in love, affected a man's potency. Men and women lived in harmony with the rains that washed across the valley.

Rita's body is like the earth, he thought, enjoying her hands moving on his body, hearing her moan, a warmth and moistness ready to receive him. I am the rain. Our perfume of love will be the fragrance of rain and earth.

Rain from Mexico tinged with the flavor of mangos, strong coffee, the call of vendors in the mercado. It was the soaking kind of rain the earth needed after the long, hot month of June. It would lie like a blanket over the valley and the mountain, oven the entire state for a few days, and it would renew the scorched earth.

"Amor," Rita whispered, and he turned and drew her to him.

"Rain at last," he answered her, and the sweet mixture in the room held her aroma, her perfume like the red cactus flowers of the desert, fruit flavor of the roses that grew in her garden, everything opening and exuding its soul to receive the rain, as Rita would receive him.

The flavor of the roses would change to sweet apricot as the rain kissed the petals, as the perfume of Rita's body would change when his body covered hers. The piñon scent of the incense she burned would mix with the sweat of love, and love would create meaning under the blanket of the cool night.

"How do you feel?" she asked, caressing his chest.

"I feel like making love to you," he replied, and they kissed.

"Ven," she said, and moved toward the bed.

He followed, thinking, I'm okay, I'm okay, everything's going to be just fine. He sat on the edge of the bed to take off his boots and pants. She reached out and embraced him. Her body made the hair on his arm rise, a soft, welcome tightness washed over his stomach and thighs. He breathed deep as he pressed his face into the cleavage of her breasts.

❧ REINALDO ARENAS ❧

The Color of Summer
or The New Garden of
Earthly Delights

Reinaldo Arenas was born in Cuba in 1943 and escaped to the United States during the Mariel boat lift in 1980. At the time of his death from AIDS in 1990, his poems, essays, plays, and eight novels had established his reputation as an excellent (and un-mistakably original) writer. This is "The Areopagite's Story" from The Color of Summer *or* The New Garden of Earthly Delights.

THE STORY OF RUBÉN VALENTÍN DÍAZ MARZO, THE AREOPAGITE, like the story of every petty criminal, is a pathetic one. When he was a little boy, if his parents wanted to screw without him around they would just throw him out of the house, so the poor little thing would have to sit out on the porch and listen to his parents' moan-ing—or more often, the racket they made as they slapped and yelled terrible insults at each other. As a teenager, while his mother was in bed with one of the neighbors (his father would be away on militia duty), Rubén was raped on the porch by a vagrant, then by a black man, and then—horrors!—by an old hag with huge tits who practically suffocated him not only with her tits but with her cunt as well, since she sat on Rubén's face and made the poor thing eat beaver-pie. Then when he was a young man his parents fled to the United States, leaving him behind; since he was of military age, it was against the law for him to leave the country. And it was that same law that forced him into Obligatory Military Service, where in less than a month he'd been passed from hand to hand (i.e., raped) by his entire platoon, including the lieutenant and the head of the Political Section. Terrified and half dead, reeling from this dreadful experience, Rubén escaped from the camp and negotiated the *permuta* that we mentioned earlier, which left him not only swindled (because he never received the money that was coming to him) but thrown into the world to suffer even further outrages in his two-room "suite" in the Hotel Monserrate—for there, Mahoma, SuperSatanic, Coco Salas, Mayra the Mare, and all the other aging whores in the building immediately forced Rubén Valentín Díaz Marzo to screw them. Even one of Fifo's foreign spies, who came into Cuba on a diplomatic passport and had an *unbelievable* potbelly, commanded the young man to "take her." And to top off the humiliation, the spy, who signed her name "Anastasia Filipovna," turned out to be a military officer in drag.

It was only to be expected, then, that the young man should develop an incurable sexual block. He would have liked to make love, he knew he would enjoy the act of sex, but he couldn't do it. The only way he could enjoy sex was by watching other couples screw—and from a certain distance even then since Fifo had handed down a law that punished peeping toms severely.

Thus, Rubén Valentín Díaz Marzo would go off to the parks in Havana, climb up in the leafiest tree he could find, and peek

through the foliage at the benches on which lovers would be fren-
ziedly making love. Then, protected by the foliage, Rubén would
masturbate. It was only thus, sitting amidst the shady branches of
a tree, that he could reach orgasm. And by now there wasn't a tree
in the entire city of Havana that the *Areopagite* hadn't climbed up
and jerked off in. Yes, the Areopagite because so famous were his
aerial masturbations as he looked down upon any sort of couple at
all—men with women, tops with bottoms, German shepherds with
midgets, vagrants with police chaplains—that Rubén Valentín Díaz
Marzo had at last acquired that nickname—which was really more
an honorific, or a title, than some tacky *nickname*. But the Areopagite would never be capable of making love to any of those bodies
that writhed in pleasure as he secretly gazed upon them. He had
to content himself—for such was the nature of his block—to watching, and to cumming all alone, among the leaves. He was, then,
condemned to be the the Areopagite for the remainder of his poor
complex-ridden life!—Jesus! St. Nelly! Could anything be sadder
than a poor man who can taste sexual pleasure only by spying on
the pleasures of others?

Yes, sad indeed, my dear, is the Areopagite's story. Sometimes
he had to sit on a tree limb for hours on end, waiting for a luke-
warm couple to heat up enough for the boyfriend to lift his girlfriend's skirt and the girlfriend to grab her boyfriend's member. No
matter that rain soaked him to the skin, that sometimes lightning
hit the very tree he was perched in, that the wind buffeted him in
his nest—the Areopagite would cling to his branches with the stub-
bornness of a lizard. . . . My tears flood the page as I write the Areopagite's tale, which I have heard his very lips, terrified and
trembling, tell in a wrenching voice of loneliness, despair, and

forever-unsatisfied longing. His is a sadness born of the horror and baseness of the present age. The poor Areopagite would madly hump the trunk of a spruce tree, a bully tree, a haya tree, a bay laurel tree, a thorny ceiba, or a swaying pine tree, and to muffled sighs and weeping he would at last ejaculate, while the impassioned lovers down below would actually, deliciously, couple.

Dear lord, and if to this we add the dire risks and near-fatal pratfalls that his erotic adventures sometimes entailed, then surely the reader will see how truly and terribly wretched the Areopagite's life was. For instance, sometimes the uncontainable arc of his se-men would fall from the heights down onto the face of a lover, who would indignantly discover the peeping tom above, grab rocks and sticks and anything else he could find, and hurl them furiously at the Areopagite, who would make his escape (by leaping from tree to tree) only at the risk of a fall that could easily break his leg, or even his very neck. But at other times, the Areopagite would actually bring other people pleasure. Once, for instance, after a young lady had spent hours futilely sucking an impotent soldier's cock, the Areopagite solved the problem when his stream of warm cum fell into the young woman's face, naturally leading her to think that it was the soldier's and that she had at last succeeded. She embraced her soldier in an ecstasy of pleasure, and from then on the couple always went to the same bench, where the Areopagite could generously bathe the young woman's face with his love liq-uor. But mishaps occurred more often than successes. Many times as he came he would almost swoon, and he would lose his balance. At that, he would crash down out of the tree onto the impassioned lovers, who, enraged, would usually give him a double beating — for the physical damage he'd caused by falling on them and for the coitus interruptus. . . . Once the Areopagite made such a racket up in the tree that he was discovered by an army lieutenant whose meaty member was being deep-throated at the time by Carlitos Olivares, the Most In-Your-Face Queen in Cuba. The lieutenant, thinking that the Areopagite was a spy who'd report him to that jealous bitch Raúl Kastro, pulled out his pistol and, to the desperate shrieks of Carlitos, who thought she was about to be murdered, blasted away at the treetop. It was a miracle that Rubén got out of that one alive, I'll tell you. And another time, when a bunch of students were having a little circle-jerk under a tree in Central Park, the Areopagite came crashing down on them and smashed several of their erect members flat; they almost kicked him to death. Another time, in Lenin Park, the Areopagite lost his grip on a huge rubber tree under which a hundred scouts in the Camilo Cienfuego troop of the Followers of Ché Guevara had formed a delicious daisy chain. The ensuing fall broke not only the daisy chain but the bones of the poor Areopagite as well, who in spite of his injuries had to make his escape before the scouts could pull up their shorts and stone him to death.

Over time, the Areopagite conceived a special voyeuristic fantasy—he dreamed of climbing up into the rafters of the Garcia Lorca Theater and jerking off while Azari Plizeski or Jorge Esquivel made love to Halisia Jalonzo, naked, in her dressing room. To fulfill this fantasy, he sought Coco Salas's help, and at last, after making all manner of promises to Coco (even going so far as pledging to make the Key to the Gulf Coco's own personal and exclusive sex slave), he was allowed to climb up into the heights of the theater, from where he could look down into Halisia's dressing room. That night, like almost every night, Halisia hobbled out on her crutches to the middle of the stage (this was just an ordinary performance—no mosquitoes) and danced *Giselle*. At one of the ballet's most romantic moments, when Giselle was dancing with that gorgeous prince with the big basket, Halisia whirled offstage for a moment, stuck her hand into her cunt, pulled out a bloody Kotex, and then did a marvelous (and most uncommon) jeté into the arms of the prince—to deafening applause. Oh, but the desperate Areopagite, who was hoping for something a bit more erotically inspiring, was so disappointed that he lost his grip on the rope he was hanging on and fell onto the stage—at the precise moment the entire corps de ballet had encircled the lovers in a beautifully choreographed scene. Leaping off the stage, the Areopagite tried to escape, but Fifo's implacable police, tipped off by the all-knowing midgets, grabbed him before he could get away.

So now the Areopagite is awaiting trial for contempt, sabotage, and personal damages—crimes punishable by up to eleven years in prison and a thousand rations of five pesos each. And Skunk in a Funk, the Areopagite's friend and confessoress, has promised to intervene for him. This very afternoon, in fact, Skunk has an appointment with Bias Roka at the Palace of Justice. Oh, yes, she was going to speak to Bias, whose prick the Skunk had sucked once in an elevator when she was on her way to the courtroom to be tried for corrupting the morals of a minor. Once again she would get on her knees before the old militant in the Communist Party Central Committee, kiss his shriveled balls—all that and *much more* the poor Skunk would do to save that poor, long-suffering Areopagite from prison. For once in prison, what tree or statue was the poor voyeur ever going to be able to climb in order to get his rocks off? Yes—she, Skunk in a Funk, was willing to perform the most *ap-*

palling sacrifices, even go so far as to suck Bias Roka's cock, or Felipe Carnedehado's, even to screw Alfredo (Güé) Güevavara — anything, everything — she would do it all if it would free the poor lonely Areopagite, *son frere, son semblable,* from the claws of justice. . . . Yes, but first I've got to go over to Clara Mortera's house — she gave me an ultimatum, and I've got to run over to her room on Wall Street in time for that meeting. My heavens, what's gotten into that creature? And the worst part of it is that I can't say I'm not going because in addition to being such a horrid sinister old woman she's a genius, and *mon semblable,* too — plus she'd done me no end of favors. So I'll go. Then we'll see about Bias.

⊲ ANA CASTILLO ⊳

Peel My Love Like an Onion

*Someone referred to Julia Alvarez as "a one-woman cultural col-
lision." The same could be said for Ana Castillo. She is a prolific
poet, novelist, and critic. In this scene from* Peel My Love Like an
Onion, *her protagonist, a flamenco dancer with one bad leg re-
sulting from childhood polio, gets a much deserved foot massage.*

SOMETIMES WHEN I GET ON THE TRAIN I LEAN MY HEAD AGAINST
the window, close my eyes and let myself remember Agustín, who
was not dark like Manolo, but cream-colored like vanilla. But not
sweet—never sweet. When I remember Agustín I am not so tired.
I no longer smell the grease in my hair, or hear the echo of the
deafening airport noises, loud pages over the intercom all day long,
bla-bla of everybody talking at once, moving moving, beep-beep of
those little carts with the flashing yellow light on top carrying people who are going away someplace, career people with business
accounts and nice luggage and people who have vacations and take
them, and me meanwhile tossing little frozen pizzas into a hot oven
from 2 p.m. till 9 eight days a week like the Beatles used to sing
and Mexicans still say.

33

Most of the time I pretend I don't speak English so that I don't have to answer to customers.

On the train ride home, sometimes, not always, I think of Agustín and his pale gray eyes, sad like a rain cloud, and bushy reddish-blond eyebrows, and I smile myself into a little nap. Six stops until I get off, with long clankety-clank time between them. My feet are always burning from holding me up for seven hours a day; feet that used to dance in heeled shoes, that ached with pleasure from doing what they did so well, feet that, if they never made me a rich woman, at least paid my rent. Feet that Agustín caressed.

Now they are just feet.

I liked Agustín's feet, too, although I rarely saw them. Once or twice he stayed until the morning and I caught a glimpse of them when he came out of the bathroom. Usually it was night and dark in my room or in his room when he took off his shoes. They were very white, waxy-looking, like those figures with the glass eyes that they exhibit in wax museums, smooth, smooth, without blemish or lines anywhere. Never a bunion or callus. How could a man's feet be so flawless? Agustín's wax feet looked like they'd melt in the sun. But I liked them and the tiny blondish-red hairs that grew wild on his toes and at the very top of each foot. There were only a few from what I remember. But it was just a glance or two I ever had of those feet. He didn't know I noticed. So the second time I glimpsed Agustín's feet, I said, ¡Mira! tus pies! Because this time I wanted the chance to hold them as he had often held mine after rehearsals in front of everybody. I wanted to marvel at his perfect feet as he marveled over my very imperfect pair.

Why should I look at my feet? he asked. What's wrong with them? He glanced down and noticing nothing out of the ordinary for him went on with his grooming. They're beautiful, I said. He laughed. He laughed and ran his hand in a self-conscious gesture through his thinning hair. Men don't have beautiful feet, he said. Oh, what do you mean? I insisted. Men can have beautiful feet. *You* have them! Estás loca, he said. And that was all we ever said about feet.

Except when he massaged mine, held them tight on his lap when we had done a show and it had gone well and the snifter was filled to the brim with tips and we had all the cognacs and fans and new friends and we managed to get envidia from those who wished for our moment in the spotlight but were sitting in the sidelines, in the dark, getting drunk and whispering mean things about Agustín and me, Agustín would say it didn't matter because they were just jealous and could not ever perform as well as we. Not even in their dreams, he said. Although what we think is life is only a dream, anyway, he would add. When Agustín held my feet in his maestro's hands, hands not as perfect as his feet but far more gifted, I felt that more than money, more than all the champagne in the world, all the silk costumes and pañuelos and brocaded shawls and gold bangles, more than all the lovely things I so rarely got a chance to touch, to own, to try—to feel Agustín's skillful hands, the same that played his guitar in such a way that was not playing but something beyond me to put into mere words, something like fire and a waterfall at the same time, this was . . . but of course if I am going to try to describe it at all it has to be in terms of nature, that is wise at all times, not brujo's magic that sometimes backfires, not skill which anyone can acquire, but fiery orange blazes and thunderstorms all at once. And I am saturated by both. To have those same hands holding my feet and bringing each one up to his lips for a soft kiss, and placing one against his cheek and then the next, oh, I go to sleep on the hot train with the broken air conditioning, remembering that more than anything in the world my feet earned me the greatest happiness the rest of me has ever known.

❧ CARLOS CERDA ❧

To Die in Berlin

Carlos Cerda is considered one of the best Latin American "Boomerang" writers, having lived in exile in East Germany from 1973 to 1985, while a military dictatorship ruled his native Chile, only to return after its fall. His novel, To Die in Berlin, *from which the brief bathroom scene is taken, is one of the most intelligent and poignant works on the condition of exile ever written.*

MARIO'S AND EVA'S HABITS COINCIDED, AND THAT WAS GOOD, AND better yet was the fact that they had managed to coincide in such a short time. In effect, they had accepted one another from the very first night. When evening fell—in Berlin in winter it was already quite dark out—Eva would enter the bathtub like a peacock in a beauty salon. It's not that Eva was pretentious. She simply liked the no-excuses solitude of her bath, the water's warmth as it filled the tub, and the profusion of bath salts, colognes, and creams which delayed her subsequent entrance onstage, when Mario had already set the table with Hungarian wine and slices of sturgeon that mysteriously appeared in the house—or rather in the refrigerator—every time her parents came to visit. He usually returned home punctually from the university around seven, after his customary stroll along the bridges on the Spree. At that hour Eva was almost always in the bath while he devoted himself to organizing the dinner delights. He was meticulous with the candles, with the cheese—which had to be at room temperature, like the wine—and with the culinary surprise of the evening, sometimes a piece of pickled fish or those slices of beef tongue which he marinated in almond sauce. It was also their custom to get together to inform each other of the day's events. Mario would enter the steamy bathroom and kneel down beside the tub. Their kiss was a warm moistness, slippery, different, and then he would gaze at Eva's body, her rounded beauty beneath the transparent warmth of the water, that calm closeness telling him about her day. Eva was tiny; she was lovely in the water, a fish floating free in her natural habitat, and when she turned to take the glass of vodka (opaque in its iciness) that Mario placed within her reach—that small offering to enter into her intimacy—her legs stirred the water, her breasts seemed to grow with the little swell, and her arm rose up dripping off the excess, the gift of her slippery perfection, that shining initial toast of the evening. But the offering Mario made in order to penetrate the intimacy of Eva's bath wasn't just some vodka in a glass straight from the freezer. There was also the ritual of the gifts: Mario arrived each afternoon with something unexpected, although the frequency made it increasingly difficult to surprise her with something new. An antique salt shaker, a book about to be published, a piece of cake, a flower, a minimalist poem written on the subway, some bath salts: modest offerings in the moist, warm intimacy of the bath.

Chicano Chicanery

Daniel Chacón was born in California and graduated from CSU-Fresno and from the University of Oregon. Currently, he lives in Minnesota and teaches at Southwestern State University. This excerpt from "Andy the Office Boy" comes from Chicano Chicanery, *his debut short story collection.*

ALL THE LAWYERS AGREED, ANDY'S LOYALTY SHOULD BE RICHLY rewarded in the form of a Christmas gift. They chose Rachel Garcia, the youngest and newest of the attorneys, a recent Harvard graduate, to take up the collection. Carrying a cigar box around the floors of the firm, she managed to get fifty dollars from each of the partners, twenty-five each from the attorneys, and ten dollars each from the paralegals and secretaries, so after a week of soliciting, she had collected $780. No one knew how much she had collected, nor did they care what she got him — "Something nice," they told her — so, embittered for being asked to do such a menial job, after having graduated at the top of her class, she walked to the parking garage in the drizzling snow, pulling her coat over her face like a vampire, tempted to suck a commission from the total. Perhaps, she thought, her black eyes glittering with ideas, she should spend a hundred bucks on a nice dinner, a bottle of red wine, a seafood appetizer. Guilt, however, reminded her of Andy.

He was a skinny blonde boy with a degree in English from SSU in southern Minnesota. He would walk into her office after knocking lightly on the doorframe, carrying a bag heavy with her deli order, which he had run across the street to get for her, and he refused to keep the change. He always brought his own lunch to work, peanut butter and jelly and a Snickers bar. He never ate downtown, because, he always said, Who can afford to eat out on an office boy's salary? She remembered how he had told her, with bright blue eyes, how he had wanted to go to Boston to be a bartender in a sports bar—just like Sam Malone—but he only made it as far as Minneapolis because his ex-girlfriend got pregnant and a court ordered that he support the kid.

The cold night air stung Rachel's face. She felt the $780 in her pocket, not as if it were heavy, but as if it were a warm throb inside her jacket, like a living heart.

She walked along the Nicolette Mall, the windows displaying expensive winter coats and boots and sweaters. On her salary, 43K, she couldn't buy nice things, not because it was bad starting pay for a recent graduate, or poor pay for a single girl living in the Twin Cities, but because she lived in a condo with parking in uptown and she drove a new SUV. Plus, she paid three hundred dollars a month in student loans, so that after all her checks were written, she felt like a pauper, as if she were still in law school. The feeling that she should spend some of Andy's gift money, something, anything, made her hungry to spend it.

Who was that boy anyway and why did the lawyers like him so much? He had a kind of sickly smile, like he was dying of cancer, and his eyes darted about as if they were too eager to land on one spot. Quite frankly, he spent much of his workday at the secretary's desk e-mailing friends and family, or trying to flirt with the file clerks who pushed carts in and out of offices handing out manila folders, girls barely eighteen, with thin hips and eyes fat with ambition. They always said, "No, Andy," without even looking at him.

Why did the lawyers like him so much? Maybe simply because he was Andy the office boy, and after two years with the firm, it was clear that he wanted no more out of life than being Andy the office boy, no more dreams of bartending in Boston, no thoughts of graduate school or becoming a professional in any field. He was the one person in the firm, perhaps the one person she now knew — having been at Harvard the last three years — who wanted nothing more than to wake up every morning being who he was and doing what he would do that day. He was not a simpleton, but he was simple.

Was it a good idea, she thought, walking into the warm belly of the City Center Mall, to give such a humble boy a $780 gift? The possibility that it could corrupt him, that it could remind him that there was a material world, could take away a quality about him, something she liked to refer to as Euro-American noble savagery. He was, to her, the essence of rural Minnesota. As the junior member of the firm, she performed the unwanted duty of driving south of the Cities into the prairie, to do research with clients in towns like Gibbon and Gaylord and Renville, and one time she stopped in Marshall, Andy's hometown, where she walked into the Wooden Nickel for dinner, a pub packed with people she was sure were Andy's relatives and friends, thick Norwegians and Germans drinking beer and eating popcorn. So many of those blue eyes strained to see through the sunlight, to see her standing in the open door, a Chicana with a briefcase.

She tried on sweaters and skirts and pants and coats and about twenty pairs of shoes, longing to buy something, just one thing with the money meant for him. Her clothes, although professional and smart looking, had fading fringes. She had only gotten a few paychecks so far, and she had no savings and her three credit cards had been maxed out in law school. Her parents were no help because together they made far less than what she made. They still rented an apartment on a dark, narrow street in downtown El Paso. She didn't dare tell them how much she earned because they would think it was a lot and might expect her to send money home.

In Saks Fifth Avenue, she tried on a baby-blue cashmere sweater, so soft on her flesh that it seemed like a feather massage. She saw herself wearing that sweater, walking the offices of the firm with confidence and power and the knowledge that people were noticing her. It cost $550. She handed it to the salesgirl and said, "No, thank you."

The snow let up and she walked downtown for several blocks. She passed cafes, bars, jazz clubs, and nice restaurants, all of them full of happy people. What she saw next stopped her walk. It was a three-story brick building with a bright red neon sign hanging down the side. "Sex World."

She had been so focused on law school and now on work that she let no one near her, and, not being good at casual sex, she had gone without it for almost four years. Seeing the flashing lights of Sex World, desire gnawed at her, not because she felt stimulated by pornography—she felt it demeaning and exploitative and ugly—but because the letters *s.e.x.* and the concrete action that those letters represented caused her to feel the full weight of her loneliness.

She entered Sex World, relieved to see couples and young women among the shoppers. The first floor had videos fitting most fetishes, and there were peep shows in the back. She was looking at the video boxes when she heard a familiar whine. It was Andy the office boy, saying to the clerk, "More change. More change." She furtively followed him and saw him go into a booth. The young lawyer heard the door lock. Then she heard him say, "Yes. Nice. Nice."

When the day came to give Andy his gift, all the lawyers gathered in the main office and said, "Surprise!" as the office boy walked in. He smiled broadly and waved at everybody. Everyone turned to Rachel Garcia. One lawyer said, "The gift."

The young lawyer cleared her throat. "Andy," she said, "this is from all of us. We collected money from everyone and got you this."

"Show it," they said. "Let him have it."

"But," she said, "it's too big to drag around. So come with me. They all know what it is," she said, and the lawyers agreed, because it would seem insensitive to not know what they had gotten him.

"We'll be right back," she said.

And everybody said, "Of course," as if they had arranged it that way.

She led him into the conference room. "Sit down," she said. He nervously sat. To Andy's astonishment, the pretty lawyer undid the buttons of her baby-blue cashmere sweater.

"Oh," he said, watching her pull it down her smooth, dark shoulders. "Nice. Very nice," he said.

◄[DENISE CHÁVEZ]►

Face of an Angel

Denise Chávez, a native of Las Cruces, New Mexico, has written short stories and plays, taught both creative writing and theater, as well as touring America with her one-woman performance piece, Women in the State of Grace. *This wise and witty advice about men comes from her debut novel,* Face of an Angel.

Talks with Dedea I: Los que se presentaron

Dearest Dedea:

Men will present themselves. It's a given. Before. During. Or after work. Take everything in stride as you would a wrong order. Instead of con queso, you get guacamole. Men can be like that guacamole. A nice appetizer, a little spicy, but not a full-course meal.

Don't put too much stock in men. They will have to prove their mettle. Are they serious contenders? Many men will flirt with you. How you respond is what matters.

I have never had trouble with men bothering me at El Farol (well, except Albert Chanowski, but that's another story). I attribute this to the fact that I approach my customers in a friendly but businesslike manner. We are not here to fraternize with our clients, remember that. Nothing is sloppier or less professional than a waitress who pals around with her customers. When I am working, I work. As much as I love my customers like Bud Ermin and Whitey Moldon, Bosford and Nayla Comingly, Billy Jane and Mr. Tangee, I leave them behind when I go home. I don't socialize with them after work. I don't need to, I see them every day. They know how I am and what to expect from me, and as a result, we are friends.

Don't have any expectations of your customers. You have to allow for changes in mood and attitude. If you don't, you will soon be disappointed.

Hungry people are grouchy. People who don't know you can be rude. Those that know you can be demanding and selfish. I approach my customers with a sense of unspoken propriety and, in return, they are polite to me.

The only person who has crossed the proverbial line at work is Albert, and he is teetering dangerously on the edge. All his life, women have catered to him. With me, he is off-guard, off-center, and to him that is very attractive. He's not a dangerous man, but he is unpleasant.

Stay away from these men. If they bother you, tell me or Larry or switch with someone who can handle and control them. Pancha understands men and how they work. Rely on her and Melina Minao. They've both been married and divorced and married and divorced and they know what to do about any number of types of men. Ignore crude and crass jokes, the hello-honey syndrome, sexist endearments.

Stay away from people who touch you. Comport yourself with dignity. You are a waitress, and what you reap you will sow.

Many will call, but few should be chosen. In time you will understand what I mean.

I mean like César Fuentes will call upon you at home on an off-night. They will be drinking, as César did, for that is the only way such men can find the strength to present themselves to you. Tall, with perfect posture, he was a teacher at Agua Oscura Junior High, where he taught seventh grade. He was an older man who used to come into the restaurant. He was never my teacher, or even Hector's, but I got to know him over the years. He came in first with his wife, Vina, and then later alone. Vina got cancer of the uterus and she was confined to her bed. César was always very gentlemanly, proper, polite. He barely seemed to notice me, and I felt sorry for him.

"That's where it begins. Soveida, you better watch out!" declared Pancha Portales.

"I do feel sorry for him, a man in his early sixties, so tall and straight, without a woman to love him," I said.

"THE OLDER YOU GET, THE MORE YOU SEE MEN LIKE CÉSAR, WITH crippled wives, or wives who can't make love ever again because of their womb, or tubes or cervix or back. And as a result, it goes without saying, it goes. The man's penis shrinks to the size of a small thumb."

"César never told me about his wife, Pancha. How do you know about her?"

"I know these things. The gringa's got her sex cut out and still she's sick inside, Soveida. Cesarito don't get it no more. It's been that way for over fifteen years. I say he should find himself someone for companionship."

"Pancha Portales!"

"I do! He's still got huevos underneath that brown cowboy suit and hairy legs in those Tony Lama boots, enough to put round some woman, if you just cover up his face. It's not that he's ugly, he's not.

It's just that there's something hard about him. It would be like making love to your grandfather's death mask. But just get a dark room and the plaster-of-Paris look will go away."

"Pancha!"

"I mean it, Soveida. He needs a woman and soon. The longer this goes on, the straighter his back becomes. One of these days he's just going to snap apart or turn into a statue. Híjole, he already has! What he needs is a good woman to unloosen his calzones, they're cutting off his circulation."

"Pancha!"

"When I was single, married men never interested me at all. Who wants someone else's day-old beans? Not that the single ones aren't damaged as well. When you come right down to it, give me flowers and a little romance and then go on your way, that's what I tell my men. I don't want to brag, Soveida, but I know more about men than Eloisa knows about green chile. Once you learn a few basic principles and the variations, you'll have it all down. Sometime when we're not so busy here at work I'll give you a few tips. You could use them."

I NEVER DID TELL PANCHA THAT ONE NIGHT CÉSAR SE PRESENTÓ, as Mamá says—he just showed up at my door. The house was very clean, Chata had just left, and César didn't quite seem himself. He was slightly disheveled, his light brown hair flecked with white and fluffed around his ears like muffs. I made a mistake and let him in. Frankly, I can't remember what César said. He mumbled rather incoherently, and then paced around the living room apologetically, then tried to kiss me. I could smell liquor on his breath. His lips were very wet, as if he had been hypersalivating. It was then I noticed his lips for the first time. Large, slightly chapped, they were the color of calf's liver. That's when I asked him to leave. He seemed so unlike the other César. This new César seemed so infinitely sad, I wished I could have held him, but I couldn't. Just as apologetically as he came in, he left, still mumbling, moving a moist tongue around his veiny mouth. We never spoke of that night, but I have wondered all the rest of my life what possessed César, and how he could have mustered the strength of will to present himself. There was something heroic about it.

"*IF IT WEREN'T FOR HIS FACE LIKE A CHEAP PAPIER-MÂCHÉ MASK and those eyebrows like a chipmunk's tail,*" *Pancha said.*

"*And his meaty lips,*" *I answered.*

"*Yeah, I noticed them, too. If it weren't for those things, I might once have thought about it, Soveida,*" *Pancha stated firmly.*

"*Pancha!*"

"*I mean it! A woman has her needs. But let me tell you, men like César are to be avoided. You had César, I had Juanito Tafoya. Eulalia, his wife, weighed three hundred pounds. I call those men the Shipwrecked. They'll cling to you because they're drowning. God forbid you sleep with them, they'll spend a good ten minutes nursing at your breasts and then fall asleep. They usually snore, too. It isn't that they're not equipped, they just got too waterlogged over the years, if you know what I mean. You can't get rid of them either, they're like seaweed.*"

Many will call, but few should be chosen.

So avoid anyone who is drunk, Dedea, or married, and who tries to kiss you against your will.

＊　　＊　　＊

"Type number two, Soveida: the Fake He-Man. Sylvester Stallone with a girdle. Robert Goulet with a truss. What's his name puss pussycat-pussycat without a meow. Now, I once went out with a gringo, yes, I did, nothing wrong in that, I was foot-free and fancy-loose. What I didn't know was that he used hair spray, and he also painted his nails with clear polish. I didn't find out about his dentures until late one night on the couch at my apartment. Well, I got him out of there faster than you can say Bionic Man. Artificial men are afraid of real women. They don't like the way we smell. They're afraid of menstrual blood. I blame their mothers. They care more about the way their fingernails look than they'll ever care about you. They're selfish in bed, too. They like to get chupados. You'll be sucking on a dead stick all night long. So forget them, Soveida."

"Pancha!"

"I mean it, if you have the time to resurrect Lazarus, go ahead and do it."

Shun men with wives who are incapacitated with female problems, have cancer, or are fat, Dedea. Steer clear of men who are rigid, tight-skinned, thin-lipped, straight-backed, unbending, have no sense of humor, and who flirt too easily and too much, especially in front of other women.

"Let's talk about small-penis men, Soveida. There are several types. The Small No-Can-Do and the Small Can-Do. One of

my favorite honeys was a short—in height—cowboy trucker named Squirty Boysville. Where'd you think I learned to dance country, Soveida?

"A man of the land, he called himself. Well, he knew land and he knew land. Just because he had small albóndigas, little meatballs, didn't mean he couldn't simmer the soup to a boil. The man you have to look out for is not the small link sausage but the Jimmy Dean deluxe. They're usually good kissers. Period. I call them Mr. Hit-and-Miss. Give me my 5'2" Squirty any day."

NEVER LET DOWN YOUR GUARD, DEDEA. STAY AWAY FROM THE EX-husbands of relatives. Evade any men with women attached. Most men have some woman or women attached. Mothers (the worst scenario). Ex-wives (very bad). Daughters (terrible). Old lovers they can't emotionally release (unbearable).

Every woman knows men on the make, whether they're drunk or, worse yet, sober, who after circling the block pause, falter, and then gather themselves up for their passionate confessions. But don't succumb!

"SOVEIDA, HAVE I MENTIONED MR. EVERYTHING IS BUSINESS, EVEN that? He's usually a bad tipper with a dry mouth. There's also Godzilla, into power, like that creep Albert Chanowski. Voyage ripens, he wants women to wait on him. What about the Love Me I'm an Artist, tall, good-looking, with long legs and quick ejaculations? Or Mr. Regular Dollar Tip. A businessman, usually wears a suit and tie. Likes to make jokes with the waitresses, everybody knows him, *nobody likes him. Like sleeping with a piece of toast. After being with them awhile, they start to make you itch. That's just a few types to avoid. As they come up or out around here, Soveida, I'll point them out to you. I haven't lived in this world fifty-two years for nothing, and been married three times without learning that when I found me Pheromone Fernández I'd met a Born-Again born-for-bed. He's a gentleman, to boot. But that's all I'm going to say. To me, the bedroom is sacred."*

"I feel sorry for Dedea, Pancha. She's so young, and so dumb."

"She'll learn. The way we learned. I don't feel too sorry for her. I feel sorry for all the men," Pancha said. "I mean, look at them, pobrecitos, they're so helpless. Get a good look, Soveida, check them out: Larry with Bonnie his wife and all his girlfriends, it's no wonder he has a bad heart. There's Bud and Whitey, with their little-boy dreams, Jimmy the bartender with his Playboy cautions, and Level Winkle, the cook, with his bottle of Robitussin. He's addicted to cough medicine and Moth. Who knows what else. You name it. Pobrecitos tweeds, no matter what age, nationality, or color of skin. It's for us women to be strong."

"I'll never get married again, Pancha."

"Well, I don't think I could live with a man too long without us getting married. I envy you kids, today you just live together."

"It hasn't helped us."

"I didn't think so. Owe, look, here he comes!"

"Who, Pancha?"

"César, pobre de lo pobrecitos. The poor of the poor. Pro, my God! He must have found someone. He's slouching! Maybe somebody's undone those shorts!" Pancha smiled at me and I smiled back. "It wasn't me. No way!"

"Me neither."

"I don't know who it could have been, Soveida, but I'm grateful to her, whoever she was."

REMEMBER, DEDEA, MANY WILL PRESENT THEMSELVES, BUT FEW, very few should ever be chosen! Soveida

Drown

Junot Díaz was born in Santo Domingo, Dominican Republic. He received his degree from Rutgers University and an M.F.A. from Cornell. Drown, *his first book of stories, established him as a sharply observant chronicler with an original style. He currently lives in New York and is finishing his first novel.*

SHE CAME HOME IN SEPTEMBER AND BY THEN WE HAD THE PATHfinder in the parking lot and a new Zenith in the living room. Stay away from her, Cut said. Luck like that don't get better.

No sweat, I said. You know I got the iron will.

People like her got addictive personalities. You don't want to be catching that.

We stayed apart a whole weekend but on Monday I was coming home from Pathmark with a gallon of milk when I heard, Hey macho. I turned around and there she was, out with her dogs. She was wearing a black sweater, black stirrup pants and old black sneakers. I thought she'd come out messed up but she was just thinner and couldn't keep still, her hands and face restless, like kids you have to watch.

How are you? I kept asking and she said, Just put your hands on me. We started to walk and the more we talked the faster we went.

Do this, she said. I want to feel your fingers.

She had mouth-sized bruises on her neck. Don't worry about them. They ain't contagious.

I can feel your bones.

She laughed. I can feel them too.

If I had half a brain I would have done what Cut told me to do. Dump her sorry ass. When I told him we were in love he laughed. I'm the King of Bullshit, he said, and you just hit me with some, my friend.

We found an empty apartment out near the highway, left the dogs and the milk outside. You know how it is when you get back with somebody you've loved. It felt better than it ever was, better than it ever could be again. After, she drew on the walls with her lipstick and her nail polish, stick men and stick women boning.

What was it like in there? I asked. Me and Cut drove past one night and it didn't look good. We honked the horn for a long time, you know, thought maybe you'd hear.

She sat up and looked at me. It was a cold-ass stare.

We were just hoping.

I hit a couple of girls, she said. Stupid girls. That was a *big* mistake. The staff put me in the Quiet Room. Eleven days the first time. Fourteen after that. That's the sort of shit that you can't get used to, no matter who you are. She looked at her drawings. I made up this whole new life in there. You should have seen it. The two of us had kids, a big blue house, hobbies, the whole fucking thing.

She ran her nails over my side. A week from then she would be asking me again, begging actually, telling me all the good things we'd do and after a while I hit her and made the blood come out of her ear like a worm but right then, in that apartment, we seemed like we were normal folks. Like maybe everything was fine.

◁ LAURA ESQUIVEL ▷

Like Water for Chocolate

Laura Esquivel was originally a screenwriter, which might account for the success of the movie Like Water for Chocolate *but doesn't explain how she wrote such a good novel. This excerpt is taken from that book, which has over two million copies in print and has been translated into over thirty languages.*

BUT SOMETHING STRANGE WAS HAPPENING TO GERTRUDIS.

On her the food seemed to act as an aphrodisiac; she began to feel an intense heat pulsing through her limbs. An itch in the center of her body kept her from sitting properly in her chair. She began to sweat, imagining herself on horseback with her arms clasped around one of Pancho Villa's men: the one she had seen in the village plaza the week before, smelling of sweat and mud, of dawns that brought uncertainty and danger, smelling of life and of death. She was on her way to market in Piedras Negras with Chencha, the servant, when she saw him coming down the main street, riding in front of the others, obviously the captain of the troop. Their eyes met and what she saw in his made her tremble. She saw all the nights he'd spent staring into the fire and longing to have a woman beside him, a woman he could kiss, a woman he could hold in his arms, a woman like her. She got out her handkerchief and tried to wipe these sinful thoughts from her mind as she wiped away the sweat.

But it was no use, something strange had happened to her. She turned to Tita for help, but Tita wasn't there, even though her body was sitting up quite properly in her chair; there wasn't the slightest sign of life in her eyes. It was as if a strange alchemical process had dissolved her entire being in the rose petal sauce, in the tender flesh of the quail, in the wine, in every one of the meal's aromas. That was the way she entered Pedro's body, hot, voluptuous, perfumed, totally sensuous.

With that meal it seemed they had discovered a new system of communication, in which Tita was the transmitter, Pedro the receiver, and poor Gertrudis the medium, the conducting body through which the singular sexual message was passed.

Pedro didn't offer any resistance. He let Tita penetrate to the farthest corners of his being, and all the while they couldn't take their eyes off each other. He said:

"Thank you, I have never had anything so exquisite."

It truly is a delicious dish. The roses give it an extremely delicate flavor.

After the petals are removed from the roses, they are ground with the anise in a mortar. Separately, brown the chestnuts in a pan, remove the peels, and cook them in water. Then, puree them. Mince the garlic and brown slightly in butter; when it is transparent, add it to the chestnut puree, along with the honey, the ground pitaya, and the rose petals, and salt to taste. To thicken the sauce slightly, you may add two teaspoons of cornstarch. Last, strain through a fine sieve and add no more than two drops of attar of roses, since otherwise it might have too strong a flavor and smell. As soon as the seasoning has been added, remove the sauce from the heat. The quail should be immersed in this sauce for ten minutes to infuse them with the flavor, and then removed.

The smell of attar of roses is so penetrating that the mortar used to grind the petals will smell like roses for several days.

The job of washing that and all the other kitchen utensils fell to Gertrudis. She washed them after each meal, out on the patio, so she could throw the scraps left in the pans to the animals. Since some of the utensils were large, it was also easier to wash them in the wash basin. But the day they had the quail, she asked Tita to do the washing up for her. Gertrudis was really stricken, her whole body was dripping with sweat. Her sweat was pink, and it smelled like roses, a lovely strong smell. In desperate need of a shower, she ran to get it ready.

Behind the patio by the stable and the corn crib Mama Elena had had a primitive shower rigged up. It was a small room made of planks nailed together, except that between one board and the next, there were such big cracks that it was easy to see the person who was taking the shower. Still, it was the first shower of any kind that had ever been seen in the village. A cousin of Mama Elena's who lived in San Antonio, Texas, had invented it. It had a thirty-gallon tank that was six feet high: first, you filled the tank with water, then you got a shower using gravity. It was hard work carrying buckets of water up the wooden ladder, but it was delightful afterward just to open the tap and feel the water run over your whole body in a steady stream, not doled out the way it was if you bathed using gourds full of water. Years later some gringos got this invention from Mama Elena's cousin for a song and made a few improvements. They made thousands of showers that used pipes, so you didn't have to do all that damn filling.

If Gertrudis had only known! The poor thing climbed up and down ten times, carrying buckets of water. It was brutal exercise, which made the heat that burned her body grow more and more intense, until she nearly fainted.

The only thing that kept her going was the image of the refreshing shower ahead of her, but unfortunately she was never able to enjoy it, because the drops that fell from the shower never made it to her body: they evaporated before they reached her. Her body was giving off so much heat that the wooden walls began to split and burst into flame. Terrified, she thought she would be burnt to death, and she ran out of the little enclosure just as she was, completely naked.

By then the scent of roses given off by her body had traveled a long, long way. All the way to town, where the rebel forces and the federal troops were engaged in a fierce battle. One man stood head and shoulders above the others for his valor; it was the rebel who Gertrudis had seen in the plaza in Piedras Negras the week before.

A pink cloud floated toward him, wrapped itself around him, and made him set out at a gallop toward Mama Elena's ranch. Juan—for that was the soldier's name—abandoned the field of battle, leaving an enemy soldier not quite dead, without knowing why he did so. A higher power was controlling his actions. He was moved by a powerful urge to arrive as quickly as possible at a meeting with someone unknown in some undetermined place. But it wasn't hard to find. The aroma from Gertrudis' body guided him. He got there just in time to find her racing through the field. Then he knew why he'd been drawn there. This woman desperately needed a man to quench the red-hot fire that was raging inside her.

A man equal to loving someone who needed love as much as she did, a man like him.

Gertrudis stopped running when she saw him riding toward her. Naked as she was, with her loosened hair falling to her waist, luminous, glowing with energy, she might have been an angel and devil in one woman. The delicacy of her face, the perfection of her pure virginal body contrasted with the passion, the lust, that leapt from her eyes, from her every pore. These things, and the sexual desire Juan had contained for so long while he was fighting in the mountains, made for a spectacular encounter.

Without slowing his gallop, so as not to waste a moment, he leaned over, put his arm around her waist, and lifted her onto the horse in front of him, face to face, and carried her away. The horse, which seemed to be obeying higher orders too, kept galloping as if it already knew their ultimate destination, even though Juan had thrown the reins aside and was passionately kissing and embracing Gertrudis. The movement of the horse combined with the movement of their bodies as they made love for the first time, at a gallop and with a great deal of difficulty.

Eccentric Neighborhoods

Rosario Ferré was born in Puerto Rico in 1942, graduated from Manhattanville College as an English major, and obtained her master's in Spanish and Latin American literature at the University of Puerto Rico. Since she began writing in 1970, she became Puerto Rico's preeminent literary figure. This passage from Eccentric Neighborhoods *is a good example of her voice—that of an intelligent, elegant, warmly generous chronicler of cross-cultural history.*

HE WAS PASSING THROUGH MAUNABO, A LITTLE TOWN ON THE EAST coast, when he saw a young girl standing by the side of the road selling mangoes under a palm tree. The mangoes were ripe, and they shone like golden globes at the bottom of a tin pan at her bare feet. The girl was very tall, and as she stood there, she swayed in the wind this way and that, just like the palm trees behind her. Her clothes were too tight for her, and her breasts rose like perfect spheres from beneath her white cotton blouse. "Has anyone told you look like a Byzantine cathedral?" Ulises asked her, getting out of the car. "Your breasts remind me of the domes of Saint Mark's basilica, your neck of Giotto's campanile, and your arms are made

of the same bronze Ghiberti used to cast the doors of paradise."
The girl thought he was crazy and burst out laughing. "I have no
idea who those gentlemen are, but if you buy half a dozen of my
mangoes, I'll close shop and go back home. I've been standing here
in the sun all afternoon with no luck."

Tío Ulises bought all her mangoes and invited her to get into
the car. The girl did so, and Tío Ulises began to hum a song the
Trío los Panchos used to play a lot: "A *la orilla de un palmar, estaba
una joven bella, su boquita de coral, y sus ojitos de estrella, al pasar
le pregunté, que quién estaba con ella, y me contestó llorando, sola
vivo en el palmar"*— "At the edge of a palm grove I met a beautiful
girl, her lips like coral, her eyes like stars. I asked who was with
her and she answered, crying, 'I live alone among the palms.'"

After a while, Ulises asked her where she lived and the girl
pointed out a run-down establishment near Maunabo's town
square. "My father, Francisco Martínez, owns a *colmado* in town,
La Cócora de Pepe. My mother and my three little brothers live
in two rooms at the back," she said. Tío Ulises drove up to the
town square, walked into La Cócora de Pepe, and introduced himself. Then he asked the man what his daughter's name was and
learned it was Filomena Martínez.

"I want to buy everything you have in your shop," Ulises told
him. The girl's father stared at him. Tío Ulises's face seemed familiar, and before telling him to get out, Don Pepe asked him what
his last name was. When Tío Ulises said it was Vernet, Don Pepe
said he'd sell him the whole store: rum, potatoes, rice, beans, plan-
tains, yams, yucas. Ulises could even take his daughter if he wanted,
all for ten thousand dollars. A few minutes later Filomena Martínez

was sitting in Tío Ulises's convertible roadster. Ulises took her to his home in La Concordia.

Filomena loved the house. The first thing she did when she got out of the car was to take off her shoes and walk barefoot through the gate. Tío Ulises liked everything about Filomena except her name. So the next day he took her to La Concordia's cathedral, sprinkled holy water on her from the baptismal font, and baptized her Venecia Vernet. He married her before a judge, bought her a trunk full of beautiful clothes, a necklace with two hundred diamonds, and a marquise diamond ring worth half a million dollars. They traveled together to Venice, where he showed her Saint Mark's basilica, the campanile, and the Grand Canal and asked if she saw how similar she was to her namesake. Venecia laughed, but since she had always been poor and Ulises was a kind man, she didn't mind his eccentricities. When Ulises went to bed with her and began to call out Adela's name in anguished tones when they made love, Venecia felt sorry for him and treated him very gently. Eventually Tío Ulises fell in love.

Tía Venecia was a free spirit and in that respect she was very much like Tío Ulises. She had grown up almost as a child of nature in a palm-thatched hut by the sea. Her father was a *mallorquín*, a merchant from Mallorca, who had come to Puerto Rico long ago and had fallen in love with a local girl from Maunabo. Venecia had only an eighth-grade education, but she was naturally intelligent, and as soon as she was settled, she began to read everything she could lay her hands on. She taught herself to speak English and she became a charming hostess to all the bankers and businessmen of La Concordia who came to dinner when she and Ulises moved to the spectacular new house at 2 Avenida Cañafístula.

Rosario Ferré

Tía Venecia was beautiful and she knew it. Her body was lithe
and voluptuous, and with her golden skin and dark eyes she caused
a sensation wherever she went. Before she met Tío Ulises she loved
to swim naked at the beach in Maunabo at night, where — because
the continental shelf is very shallow there — waves travel long dis-
tances and pull silver manes of foam behind them. She loved to
stretch her body over the water like the bow of a violin and feel
the sea flow over her breasts and between her legs. She had had
many lovers and she would lie with them on the beach under the
stars.

After she had lived with Tío Ulises for a while Tía Venecia
realized Ulises would never be completely faithful to her. Every
time the family made a new business deal — if they needed money
for a new cement mill or if they were planning to build a new kiln
and Ulises had to go on a business trip — he would get terribly
anxious and miss Adela. Then he'd find himself a prostitute and
bury his head in her groin until he wallowed in her acrid smell,
and only then would he be able to forget his mother and make the
deal. Venecia was very understanding and didn't object to Ulises's
behavior. But she made him move to the back of the house, where
he built himself a bachelor apartment, while she kept the front of
the house to herself. The red-light district of La Concordia was
nearby, and this was very convenient because once in a while Tío
Ulises could bring a woman into the house without anyone's noticing.

Venecia didn't want to become resentful; jealousy was a petty
emotion she considered beneath her. Furthermore, she loved
Ulises, so she decided to go on living with him on the condition

that he spend at least four nights a week with her and the other three in his bachelor apartment with whomever he wished. That way she would be able to keep her dignity and also hold on to her husband. Tío Ulises was erotically very inventive, and he built a secret passageway that connected both sides of the house. There he could run naked after his wife at night, and they could search for each other, laughing and playing hide-and-seek. Every time Tío Ulises found Tía Venecia in the dark, he felt so happy he was sure he was in heaven. And after they made love, they went back to their respective suites.

❧ IRENE GONZÁLEZ FREI ❧

Your Name Written on Water

Irene González Frei is a pseudonym, so I'll have to wing it. Your Name Written on Water, *which she wrote as a student in Rome, won the award for the best erotic novel written in Spanish. But it's not just a good erotic novel in Spanish, it's a good novel period, any category, any language, any time.*

THIRTY-FIVE MINUTES LATER A TAXI PULLED UP TO THE CURB. SAN-tiago. Before he could get out, before he could even pay the fare, I jumped into the taxi. The driver looked at me, slightly shocked.

"Listen . . . ," he started. The cabbie wore thick glasses, big and round, just like the headlights of his car.

"To Barajas Airport," I commanded. We were downtown, near Atocha Station.

"Miss, please. Won't you first let the gentleman out? Then if you want—"

"Sofía," Santiago interrupted, even more put off than the cab-driver. "I don't understand. What the hell is going on with you?"

"Nothing," I spat out. "You and I get married, and that's that." I said it without realizing that I was repeating exactly what my doctor had said.

"You're out of your mind."

"Shit!" the driver exploded, breaking all rules of cabbie etiquette. "Why don't the two of you pick out your kids' names while you're at it? Why not? I've got all day to listen to a couple of lovebirds. Sure, I'm a real romantic."

"Take us to the airport, please," Santiago said, confirming my earlier request. Then, once we were on our way, he turned to me and said, "Tell me, what do you propose we do?"

I didn't answer; even I didn't know where all this was going. I rested my head on his shoulder, not really listening to all the things he was saying: I've never seen you like this before; What bug bit you, anyway, tell me? Don't think I'm going to get on the next plane just like that, you know . . .

"Hey, what are you doing?" He covered himself as if he were naked and a gust of wind had just blown off his fig leaf.

I pinched the back of his hand, a tiny, painful squeeze — "nun's pinches," my mother used to call them. First he let out a yelp, but then he let me continue. The taxi driver didn't even flinch; by now he was already used to our bizarre behavior.

I slipped my hand into Santiago's pants and reached for his penis. It appeared quite contracted, nothing like the wondrous specimen I'd had in my mouth so many nights ago. *Oh, Sofía, you're crazy,* he whispered. I began to caress it, lightly, running my fingers over the swollen veins and massaging the head beneath the thin film of foreskin. I moved my hand up and down, relaxed and calm, and then I noticed how his breathing changed, as did his *Oh, Sofía,* and I felt his penis grow larger in my hand. To move up and down my hand now had to travel a longer stretch, and the distance kept increasing. I pushed back his foreskin and out popped the red tip, rebellious thing, a vital organ if I ever saw one. I brought my fingers up to my mouth; they tasted acidic. I covered them with saliva and then brought them back down, drenching the tip of his penis, and he was murmuring *Sofía, Sofí*, the whole time, and I noticed that it was already wet. I never knew that penises could sweat—or maybe, I thought, it was my hand, from before. Anyway, what with the movement of the taxi and the warm wetness of his penis, I practically didn't have to do anything at all—the rest of it took care of itself, really: *Oh Sofí, Sofí*, etc. He seemed to be delirious with pleasure. I, on the other hand, still resting: my head against his shoulder, was not experiencing all that much pleasure, mainly because of the taxi driver, who drove on impassively. All he had to do was turn his head to the side when looking out for oncoming traffic and I'd have to look at him: not only his pimply neck and his cap, but his face, and the poor guy was pretty unattractive. He had a long, bony face and a prominent nose from which thick black hairs sprouted. They were none too pleasant, so I opted to look instead at another set of hairs. That is to say, I glanced down at Santiago's hair, from which his penis shot out, by now rather vertical, straining itself to the very limit of its possibilities.

My hand, rising and falling in quick rhythm against that hard flesh, felt almost imperceptible granules, like seeds almost, or the atoms that made up his granite penis. His neck was now arched back, his head resting against the backseat. At this point, he had lost all of his previous composure. *Sofía*, he said, *tighter, tighter*, and so I held it tight. *More Sofí, more*, and I squeezed it, I strangled it, but it still wasn't enough for him. He wet it himself, he gripped it himself, and I gripped the hand that gripped his penis. He let his pants drop down a little bit more and returned his cock to my hand alone. He then wet a finger and stuck it in his anus. *More, Sofi, more,* he gasped as he grabbed his balls and pushed his finger farther and farther in. Now, the taxi driver was beginning to get a little curious, and every so often would peer at us through the rearview mirror, without saying a word. He didn't have to, really — Santiago was saying more than enough already with all his *More, mores.* Then I got down on my knees and took his penis with both hands; it was really at its breaking point by now, an imposing, a truly formidable erection. I still was able to continue my up-and-down routine with both hands, but it was no easy task. *Come on, Sofía, come on* — he practically was shouting by now, burying even farther the finger he had inserted in his anus, and I got the message that now he was ready. With all my might I tightened the pressure around his penis, dug my nails into it, and then with a gust of energy squeezed one last time, giving it a final, violent jolt.

What followed was an ejaculation that was truly worthy of such an erection, an exuberant, impetuous stream that must have reached the ceiling of the cab, though I didn't think to look, and then spilled onto his pants and my hands. From my crouched position I looked up to see if the cabdriver had witnessed the apotheosis, which surely would have irritated him plenty. But he hadn't; luckily, at that moment the only thing on his mind was a tourist bus hogging up two lanes on the highway.

With little gasps of pain, Santiago slowly extracted his finger from his anus. Then he passed me a handkerchief, and we cleaned ourselves up as best we could, which wasn't much. I resumed my position next to him on the backseat as he attempted unsuccessfully to put his pants back on. His erection hadn't quite subsided; in fact, it looked as straight and hard as it had before. *Oh, Sofi,* he said yet again, *you're such a little tart.* I rolled down the window; it didn't smell good at all inside the cab.

"The worst thing of all," I said to him in a low voice, "is that now we don't have anything to do at the airport."

The Years with Laura Díaz

Carlos Fuentes is widely regarded as Mexico's leading novelist. He has also taught at Harvard, Princeton, and Columbia; written essays, screenplays, political journalism; and served as ambassador to France. Of his many superlative works, I've chosen a selection from The Year with Laura Díaz, *probably my personal favorite, but it's always so hard to decide.*

THE HIDALGO MADE HER A PRESENT OF A LOOK THAT COMBINED adoration with fate. That night, together in bed in the L'Escargot Hotel facing the Parque de la Lama, the two of them caressing each other slowly, over and over, cheeks, hair, temples, he asked her to envy him because he could see her face from various perspectives and, above all, illuminated by the minutes they spent together. What does the light do to a woman's face, how does a woman's face depend on the time of day, the light of dawn, morning, midday, sunset, nighttime, what does the light that faces her, outlines her, surprises her from below or crowns her from above, attacks her brutally and without warning in broad daylight or caresses her softly in the half-light, what does it say to her face? He asked her, but she had no answers, no wish to have answers, she felt admired and envied because in bed he asked all the questions that she always wanted a man to ask, knowing they were the questions that all women want to be asked at least once in their lives by just one man.

She no longer thought about minutes or hours, she lived with him, beginning that night, in a time without time of amorous passion, a whirlwind of time that dispensed with all the other concerns of life. All the forgotten scenes. Although at dawn on that night, she feared that the time with him, this night with him, had devoured all the previous moments of her life and had also swallowed up this one. She clung to the man's body, clasped it with the tenacity of ivy, imagining herself without him, absent but unforgettable, saw herself in that possible but totally undesired moment when he would no longer be there even if the memory of him was; the man would no longer be with her but his memory would be with her forever. That was the price she paid from that moment on, and she was pleased, thought it cheap in comparison with the plenitude of the instant. She could not keep from asking herself, in anguish, What does this face, these eyes, this voice without beginning or end mean? From the first moment, she never wanted to lose him.

"Why are you so different from the rest?"

"Because I look only at you."

She loved the silence that followed sex. She loved that silence right from the first time. It was the hoped-for promise of a shared solitude. She loved the place they'd chosen because it was at the same time a predestined place. The place of lovers. A hotel next to the shady, cool, and secret park within the city. That was how she wanted it. A place that might always be unknown, a mysterious sensuality in a place that everyone but lovers takes to be normal. For all time, she loved the shape of her man's body, svelte but strong, well proportioned and passionate, discreet and savage, as if the body of the man were a mirror of transformations, an imaginary duel between the creator god and his inevitable beast. Or the animal and the divinity that inhabit us. She'd never known such sudden metamorphoses, from passion to repose, from tranquility to fire, from serenity to excess. A moist, fertile couple one for the other, each one endlessly divining the other. She told him she would have recognized him anywhere.

"Even feeling around in the dark?"

She nodded. Their bodies joined once again in the free obedience of passion. Outside it was growing light; the park surrounded the hotel with a guard of weeping willows, and one could get lost in the labyrinths of high hedges and even higher trees, whose whispering voices were disorienting and could make anyone lose their way with the sound of rustling leaves in lovers' ears, so far away from what would come next, so close to what was absent.

The Agüero Sisters

In case you skipped my Introduction (Hey, I probably would've skipped it, too), Christina García is partly responsible for this anthology. I was familiar with the magic realism/boom writers, but Dreaming in Cuban *made me realize there must be other new voices in the Latin American tradition. She was born in Havana and grew up in New York City. What follows is from her second novel,* The Agüero Sisters, *which, like its predecessor, is a wonderful work of complexity, subtlety, poignancy, generosity, warmth, and lyrical richness.*

BLANCA AND I WERE MARRIED AT CITY HALL THE DAY AFTER HER graduation. It was only the two of us, the one-armed judge, and a listless witness from the state. Blanca wore a fitted carmine suit and a broad-brimmed hat with a spray of fresh violets. I found her ravishing.

For our honeymoon, we traveled to the Isle of Pines, where I had seen the great leatherback so many years before. Blanca wanted to sit on the same beach and wait for the she-turtle, convinced that it would return. We lingered night after night under a waxing moon, but the leatherback never came.

Those nights on the beach are still vivid to me, yet remote as a diorama. Our love was sheltered by the coconut palms serenaded by the low whine of insects. How slight Blanca was, ribbed like an underfed cat, but soft too, in unexpected places. Her scent was sharp and green then like budding leaves, inextricable from our passion I would lie beside her and whisper: *Estoy contento, querida.* And for a moment, time seemed to stop its audible march in our small paradise.

The Isle of Pines is scrubby, about two thousand square miles in all, and has a single languid river, Las Casas, that cuts through the capital city of Nueva Gerona. During the day, Blanca loved to wade in the river and drink from it, of questionable purity even then. I sat under the shade trees on the riverbank and watched as the water echoed off her body, overcome by the wonder of my possession.

One day, Blanca playfully coaxed me, fully dressed, into the river. When I was chest-high in the slow waters, she dove in beside me and tugged off my belt. Her boldness startled me, and I lost my footing. A force I could not fathom pulled me down and held me underwater. Just when I was certain I'd drown, I heard a child's voice imploring: Yield to the river! Yield to the river! Instead I broke free into the morning air.

Blanca emerged from the water simultaneously, sleek as a river goddess. She kissed me with a hard ardor, continuing her caresses until I surrendered to a violent pleasure. I am the river, Blanca breathed in my ear. I am the river. . . . And around us, the waters murmured assent.

Sultry Moon

Mempo Giardinelli is one of Argentina's leading literary lights. Of his many works, I've chosen an excerpt from Sultry Moon, *which topped the Argentine bestseller list for twenty-seven weeks, won Mexico's National Book Award, and has been translated into over a dozen languages.* Sultry Moon *is a thinking person's classic noir with profoundly disturbing implications.*

IT WAS IMPOSSIBLE FOR HIM TO STOP THINKING ABOUT HER, TO STOP imagining her naked. He didn't know what to do, but he had to do something. He smoked several cigarettes, many of them only halfway, and finally stood up and looked at his watch. One-thirty in the morning. What am I doing? he asked himself. I should be sleeping. But he opened the door and leaned out into the hallway again.

It was completely silent. The light was no longer coming from the half-open door of Araceli's room; the brightness of the sultry moon that entered through the window barely reached, dimly, into the hallway. He was agitated; he reproached himself for his fantasies. Children grow up, but not so fast. Yes, she had looked at him, greatly impressed, but not necessarily with the intention of seducing him. She was too young for that. She had to be a virgin, obviously, and he told himself that anything reprehensible about the situation was in his own head, in his indecent lust. But she has fallen asleep, he thought; the seductive little lamb was afraid and fell asleep. The anger he felt overwhelmed him, but there was some relief in his stomach. He crossed the hallway to the bathroom, telling himself that he would return to his room directly afterwards and go to sleep. And at that moment he heard the sound of the girl tossing and turning in her bed. He turned towards the half-open door and looked inside.

Araceli lay with her eyes closed, facing the window and the moon. She was half-naked, only skimpy panties hugged her slender hips. The tangled sheet was covering one leg and revealing the other, as if the fabric were a veiled phallus exploring her sex. She appeared to be sleeping on her left forearm, with her arms curled up around her breasts. Ramiro remained motionless in the doorway, staring at her, flustered in the presence of such beauty. He was breathing through his mouth that had become even drier, and at once he became aware of his irreversible and gradually growing erection, the trembling in his entire body.

If she had indeed been sleeping, then it must have been a restless sleep from which she easily woke up. She moved, her small breasts breaking free from the protection of her arms, and now lay face up. Suddenly she looked toward the door and saw him; she covered herself quickly with the sheet, but her right leg remained uncovered, reflecting the brightness of the moon.

They stayed like that for a few seconds, watching each other in silence. Ramiro entered the room and closed the door behind him. He leaned back against it, breathing hard, realizing that his chest was rising and then falling, rhythmically and rapidly. He was trembling but he smiled, either to reassure her or because he was so nervous. She was tense, looking at him in silence. He approached the bed slowly and sat down without taking his penetrating eyes off hers, as if he knew that that was the way to control the situation. He stretched out his hand and began to caress her thigh gently, almost without touching her. He felt Araceli tremble slightly, and he squeezed her hand, sinking into the flesh. He resettled himself on the bed, moving closer to her, retaining that kind of pathetic smile that was more like a grimace, pulled by the sudden twitch that made his left cheek throb.

"I only want to touch you," he whispered, with an almost inaudible voice, noticing the dryness of his mouth. "You're so beautiful . . ."

And without taking his eyes off her he now began to caress the entire length of her body with both hands, his eyes following the journey of his hands. They climbed up her legs and hips and came together on her stomach, climbing slowly, smoothly up her body until closing on her breasts. She was trembling, petrified.

Ramiro looked into her eyes again:

"You're so lovely," he said, and it was then that he noticed her terror, the fear that was paralyzing her. She was about to scream: her mouth was open and her eyes looked like they were about to pop out of her head.

"Don't worry, don't worry . . ."

"I . . ." she uttered, breathlessly. "I'm going to . . ."

And then he covered her mouth with his hand, stifling the scream. They struggled while he pleaded with her not to scream. He lay on top of her, pressing down on her with his body while continuing to touch her, kissing her neck and whispering to her to be quiet. And immediately, frightened but frenzied from his passion, he began to bite her lips so that she couldn't scream. He thrust his tongue between Araceli's teeth while with his right hand he probed her sex underneath her panties, and he became even more aroused upon discovering the mound of pubic hair. She shook her head, desperate to get away from Ramiro's mouth and to breathe again. It was then that, crazed and furious, he struck her with what he thought was a mild blow but which had enough force to calm her down, and she began to cry quietly even though she insisted, "I'm going to scream, I'm going to scream." But she didn't, and Ramiro let her breathe and moan as he lowered her panties and opened his pants. At the very moment he penetrated her, she let out a cry that he smothered again with his mouth. But then as Araceli started sobbing loudly, he went back to hitting her even harder, and he covered her face with the pillow while he came completely, spasmodically, inside the girl who was resisting him like a little animal, like a wounded gull. Ramiro, out of his mind, dismissing a voice that was telling him he had become an animal, uncovered the girl's face just a few centimeters and was horrified by her tearful, shattered eyes that looked at him with terror, as if he were a monster. Then he covered her face again and went back to throwing muffled punches at the pillow. Araceli struggled a while longer. It was not hard for Ramiro to restrain her, and little by little she began to calm down while he looked out the window, emotionless, without understanding, and repeated to himself that the moon was unusually sultry that night in Fontana.

⊶ FRANCISCO GOLDMAN ⊷

The Long Night of White Chickens

Francisco Goldman has written short stories and journalistic pieces (about the horrors occurring in Central America) as well as the absolute best novel about modern Guatemala, The Long Night of White Chickens. *He currently divides his time between New York City and Mexico City.*

MOYA REMEMBERS THAT FIRST MORNING, AFTER HE WOKE UP IN Flor de Mayo's bed:

"Every stroke," she said sleepily, sweetly, "feels like another, another piece of a fable, a fable that just goes on and on."

"Like another word in a fable, *mi amor?*"

"If a fable has to be made of words, *pues sí . . .* "

She was not referring to his pigeon, which now rested, salty and encrusted, wings folded, but to his hands, one of which was stroking her back and shoulders, the other stroking her *nalgas* as he held her against him. The room was warm with sunlight and love, and his touches, all the touches that were making up this one long prolongation of a sensual morning, every stroke felt to her like another "piece of a fable."

"What a pretty thought, Florcita," he said.

"On and on . . . ," she murmured.

Downstairs, as always, on and on, there was an orphanage. It didn't matter.

He stroked her *nalgas*. What pretty *nalgas*, what a pretty and perfect word, *nalgas*. One *nalga*, and the other *nalga*. Left and right *nalga*, one with a beauty mark right in the middle. Two *nalgas*, a milkier shade of brown. Very round and smooth and ample, decorated by one winking freckle right in the middle of a *nalga*, inviting so many kisses and soon delirious nuzzles. Didn't these wonderful *nalgas* express the radiant and robust side of Flor's nature, for she really was both of those things and these *nalgas* were too, warm and hearty like domed, clay bread ovens, like smooth hilltops with the sun just coming up behind, *Moya, ay no.* Her belly was charming, and her thighs smooth, strong, and long, and the triangular little puffs of flesh between her breasts and armpits always made him want to kiss them over and over before plunging his nose into the warm cow pasture clover of those armpits. As anyone can see, Moya was unspeakably happy that morning, stroking Flor's *nalgas*, prolonging her fable without words.

◦] LUCIA GUERRA [◦

The Street of Night

Lucia Guerra was born in Santiago, Chile, and is currently profes-sor of Latin American literature at the University of California, Irvine. In addition to numerous articles and books of literary crit-icism, she has written two novels as well as an award-winning collection of stories, Frutos Estranas (Strange Fruit). *This scene is from* The Street of Night, *which may be the best novel written about prostitution.*

THE LOOK IN HIS EYES WAS AS SOFT AND GENTLE AS HIS HAND ON her hair. "I never told you that I spent seven months in a detention camp. The soldiers would sometimes jerk open our cell doors after midnight . . . they tied our hands and dragged us to the patio, beat-ing us with clubs as we walked barefoot across concrete that had recently been hosed down, telling us we were going to be shot. They would blindfold our eyes, cursing us with insults about our parents, our sisters, the wives of the married men, and in the middle of these insults, they dragged us to the wall and slammed our backs against it. They even gave the order to shoot—ready, aim, fire!—but it was all a game of pretend, a game only they enjoyed, because they took pleasure in terrifying us. When they released me and I

Lucia Guerra

returned to my normal life, I found that I wasn't normal any more . . . I found that I could not fall asleep. It was impossible, because once my eyes closed, I lay there waiting for the soldiers to burst into my room and kick me out of bed. It was impossible, until I discovered that I could sleep if I left the radio on. Absurd, isn't it? But it's true, the voices of radio announcers, both men and women, were like a sedative, a tranquilizer; it was as if the ads for Escudo beer and Palmolive soap assured me that I was far away from that purgatory created by countrymen for countrymen. So, if it doesn't bother you too much to sleep with the radio on, you could spend the night here."

Meche accepted, wiping away her tears. They lay together for the next two hours, kissing and touching but going no further. Then Roberto turned on the radio and in a few minutes drifted off. She waited for his breathing to assume that rhythm of deep sleep, then she sat up quietly and stared at the young woman in the photograph. Moonlight played on the stranger's features, and it occurred to Meche that Roberto's kisses had united her with this other woman, as if they were both somehow the same person; and suddenly the lips in the photograph seemed to be smiling, the light-coloured eyes staring at Meche with an expression of profound companionship, their message indisputably clear: we are one, I live in you, my love is yours, prolonged beyond death. Meche turned to caress Roberto's feverish back, remembering the texture on the tips of her fingers of the magnolias which grew in the cemetery next to her village. In a few moments, smiling and despite the radio, she slipped into a deep and dreamless slumber.

The following morning she surfaced through sleep hearing, as though under water, the harmony of a far-off women's choir while someone nibbled at her neck and strange but gentle hands explored her naked body. Opening her eyes, she saw Roberto, felt his lips cover hers, his body sliding against her, feverish but not from any illness, while the voice of a priest began the mass; her body hot now, too, like a lake in the rainforest during a summer shower; her lips in his hair, raising up over him to offer her naked breasts, which he took in his mouth like a starving infant; and for the first time she let her hands travel down his hard body, her fingers softly combing the dense foliage of his pubic hair before they folded like petals around his thick erection. With a moan, Roberto turned her on her back and drove into her deep and hard at the moment when the priest's monotonous Latin ceased and the choir lifted their voices into another hymn; riding her even harder now, frenzied, as if his passion were a source of pain, grunting not from love but from the lash, his body wild and plunging, his tears falling on her face, as if in grief instead of delight at the end of his long and self-imposed imprisonment; she taking his head in her hands to kiss his tears away, her eyes catching sight of his dead beloved, whispering in Roberto's ear: "We are both here to love you for ever, my darling." He stiffened and slammed into her one last time, exploding as she whispered over and over, "For ever ... for ever ... for ever ..." And then it took her as an organ crashed into a series of chords and the choir voices rose distortedly over the loudspeakers of an unknown church; took her by surprise and carried her along like a tide, gasping for breath and groaning in unbelievable pleasure; pulling her along with him through a nest of heavy sea anemones and a cloud of kelp that soothed her burning body with silken tendrils; locked as one now, joined on this exquisite journey, rolling on the bed as if it were soft sand, still feasting on each other's lips as the brightly coloured lights went dim, falling as they fell into a lethargy of shared nothingness, the only kind of void where loneliness does not exist.

Dirty Havana Trilogy

Pedro Juan Gutiérrez started working at age eleven as an ice cream vendor and newsboy. By his teens he was writing poetry and fragments about his native city, and had begun to paint. This excerpt is from his Dirty Havana Trilogy, *a novel in stories, which depicts the squalor and grit (as well as the passion and joy) of modern Cuba.*

THREE OR FOUR DRINKS LATER, I HAD THE URGE TO TOUCH HER, who knows why. Well, I do know why: I had tuned out while she was talking about meals and kitchens and how her apartment shines because she's constantly scrubbing with a little rag that she always carries around with her, and that my room was a filthy pit. "A woman's touch is what you need here. I'll make it so you could eat off the floor, with some nice little curtains." As she chattered away, I was checking her out. She's forty-one, but she's fine. When I couldn't stand it any longer, I got up from my chair and I patted her head and stuck my pelvis in her face. Then she unbuckled my belt and unzipped my pants, gradually revealing my pubes and my prick, which stiffened slowly, anxiously, looking up as if to ask whether someone had called.

"Oh, Pedro Juan, what a beautiful prick. It's precious!" She said that caressingly, like it was as sweet as candy. And she took it in her mouth gently, tongue, lips, teeth, everything. Her mouth was warm and wet. She nibbled a little on the head, doing everything as if she were in a trance, her eyes closed. She persisted, rapturously, until she had swallowed all my come. All of it. She licked up the last drop.

"Let's get in bed, sweetie."

"Ugh, no, wait. Let me rest a minute."

She had sucked me dry and she wanted me to keep going like a fifteen-year-old boy.

"No waiting. You've got a tongue and fingers. After choking me to death, you can't leave me hanging. Let's go!"

She was already taking her clothes off. An incredible body! Forty-one, a diet of rice and beans, three children, and knowing nothing about creams or gyms or saunas. She was perfect.

Well, that's how it was. I poured myself another drink, and I spent a long time doing everything I could with my tongue and fingers, she panting from one orgasm to the next. At some point I recovered a little and I stuck it in her, but it wasn't very hard. I gave her a little brushwork with my prick, just like that, half-soft, on her clitoris. She panted a lot, had two more orgasms, and that was it.

"All right! Let's get some fresh air."

It was almost midnight. The roof was silent and deserted. I had managed to satisfy her. My tongue was tired, but I felt full of energy. Streaking naked like a comet from the bed to the door, I went out on the roof and there were two guys in the blue light of the full moon. They had been watching it all through a half-drawn blind, and they were tucking their pricks back in. I scared them, really startled them. They had been watching and jerking off at our expense. In a blind rage, I threw myself at them bare-fisted. They didn't have much time to react, and they were pretty scared. They were kids, and I landed a whole slew of punches, but one of them took a few steps back, pulled out a pistol, and pointed it at me.

Then I understood. They were in uniform.

"You're policemen! You fuckers, watching me and jerking off!"

The other one drew his pistol too, but my shouts had woken the neighbors and drawn them up to the roof. Naked, I kept shouting at them, but there was nothing I could do while they were pointing their pistols at me. All of a sudden one of them brought out some handcuffs. He tried to handcuff me. No one understood what was going on.

"I'll be damned if you handcuff me! They were watching us and jerking off, there through the blinds! Carmita, come out here! Carmita!"

I went into my room to put on a pair of pants. Carmita had gone. She ran downstairs as soon as she saw there was a mess with the police. That bitch! She left me high and dry!

"Citizen, you're making a public nuisance of yourself. Besides, you're exposing yourself in a public place. Come with us and let us put the cuffs on."

The neighbors jumped in.

"This isn't a public place. Who do you two think you are? And what were you doing up here at this time of night? Looking through gaps in the blinds? You've got a lot of nerve!"

Pedro Juan Gutiérrez

In a second, more than twenty neighbors had gathered and were harassing them. The officers tried to regain control of the situation, playing tough.

"Get your identification, citizen, and come with us."

"The fuck I will! I'm not going anywhere with you! Get out of here. Get out and go to hell."

The neighbors tried to calm me down. Meanwhile, the policemen opted to disappear down the stairs, because there were too many people harassing them and asking them what they were doing on the roof so late at night. They retreated, almost running, and threatening:

"We'll be back right away. You haven't seen the last of us."

They were gone and everything calmed down. The neighbors went back to their rooms and went to bed. I grabbed what was left of my ten dollars and I went down to have a beer and something to eat. In the end, things hadn't gone so badly. I got in a few punches before they drew their pistols. That was nice.

◦§ OSCAR HIJUELOS §◦

The Mambo Kings Play Songs of Love

Oscar Hijuelos is the Pulitzer Prize–winning author of The Mambo
Kings Play Songs of Love. *His other novels include* Mr. Ives'
Christmas, The Fourteen Sisters of Emilio Montez-O'Brien, Our
House in the World *and, most recently,* Empress of the Splendid
Season. *His unmistakable mix of sensuality, sweetness, poign-
ancy, lyricism, and warmth is one of the best things to happen to
recent American fiction.*

THEY SAW EACH OTHER EVERY DAY FOR TWO WEEKS. HE WOULD GO
to her house, where she rented a room from a woman there, and
they would head out into the street, a bounce in his jaunty walk.
Their love affair came down to secret moments of hurried kissing
and groping, mutual masturbation against alley walls and in movie
theaters, and this inevitably led to the consummation of this love
in a room filled with blue light by the harbor, on a bed white as
beach sand, in the apartment of a friend.

That very day he first thought of writing a canción about his
love for her. Sated and living in paradise, the younger Mambo
King, who really had never known women, thought of this lyric:

"When desire overwhelms a man's soul, he is lost to everything in the world but love . . ."

He and Maria feasted on each other for months. They'd go to a deserted stretch of beach outside Havana or to the apartment of Nestor's friend by the harbor. He never took her up to the solar he shared with his older brother, because he felt that the cheerfulness of his love would be disturbing to Cesar, who had left his wife and child, and suffered for it, too . . . And besides, what if Cesar didn't like her? His brother, his heart, his blood. In those days Nestor would rush up the stairway of their solar, his Cuban-heeled shoes tapping on the floor, passing images of himself and Maria kissing in the shadows. They'd do it on the bed and sometimes on the floor, or on a pile of dirty clothes. They seemed to love each other so much, their skin gave off a lustful heat and smell so strong that they would attract packs of wild hounds who'd follow them down the streets.

Once, when Cesar was away, she went to the brothers' flat and decided to make Nestor dinner. She was cooking up a pot of chicken and rice on the white enamel stove with animal feet, and then, ladle in hand, she stuck out her rump, pulled up her dress, and said. "Come on. Nestor."

She liked it every which way: from behind, in her mouth, between her breasts, and in her tight bottom. She would make his penis agonizingly plump and long. He used to think he would split her open, but the more he gave her, the wider she spread herself before him. He took her to the movies, where they sat in the balcony and in the midst of the crucial love scenes, he slipped one and then two and then three and then four fingers inside her. In the foyer of a building landing, he would lift up her skirt and lick her thighs. He would lean up against her like a hound, pressing his tongue against the dead center of her panties. Some days he forgot his name and where he lived and where he worked: by day at the Havana chapter of the Explorers' Club, by night in a little gambling casino nightclub called the Club Capri. She had large firm breasts. Her nipples were brown and the size of quarters, very small-tipped at first, but when he suckled them they would swell. Tiny flora of sensation blossomed and he could taste the sweetness of her milk. Livid and as thick as her wrist, his penis slid into her mouth and she reached back and opened his buttocks and stuck her hand inside, probing him. He was alive then, coño! Alive.

He was so in love with her that he could have died in her arms happily. Loved her so much he licked her rump hole. She came and he came and in the red-tinged silver-and-white that exploded in his brow and that shuddered through his body he felt a thready presence, like a soul entering him. He would lie beside her, feeling that his body had been turned into a field and that he and she floated ecstatically over that field on the wings of love. He thought about her as he scrubbed the hair-tonic stains off the back of the heavy leather chairs at his job at the club. He wore a short white jacket with three brass buttons and a little hat like a bellboy's, carried trays of food and drink to the club members and he day-dreamed about licking her nipples. Smell of linseed oil–polished wood, cologne, blue cigar smoke, flatulence. The smell of leather, hair-tonic-stained chairs, thick rugs from Persia and Turkey. Nestor laughing, Nestor happy. Nestor slapping his older brother's then-troubled back. He'd work in the little kitchen behind the bar, making crustless ham sandwiches, and drinks. He whistled, he smiled, he sang happily. He'd look out across the dining room through open French doors to the patio and garden. He would think about the devastating curvaceousness of her buttocks, the sliver of thick black hair that protruded, but just barely, from behind her spread thighs. Scent of soft violet wisteria, falling over the garden walls, leafy jasmine and Chinese hibiscus. The taste of her wide-open vagina, all red and gleaming from moistness, an open orchid to his tongue.

Waiting to see her again, he suffered through evenings when he went to work playing the trumpet and singing alongside his brother with the Havana Melody Boys. His Maria worked in the chorus line of the Havana Hilton, as one in a line of ten "beautiful cream-and-coffee-colored dancers," and that's where Nestor wanted to be, his eyes looking off not at the audience or the spotlights but into the distance. He could not help thinking about Maria. When he was not with her he was miserable, and after playing these jobs he would rush out to meet her.

For his part, Cesar was curious about this Beautiful Maria who had taken his maudlin, quiet brother and made him happy. So finally Nestor arranged that they meet one night. They chose a bar where a lot of musicians liked to go, up by Maríanao beach. *Dios Mío!* his brother Cesar was surprised by Maria's beauty and he gave Nestor his approval, but then, so did everyone else. He stood there trying like every other man to figure out how on earth Nestor had landed her. Not by know-how; his younger brother had never been a womanizer. In fact, he'd always seemed a little frightened of women. And now there he was, with a beautiful woman and a real look of happiness on his face. He hadn't won her over with his looks, pleasantly handsome, with a long matador's face and a sensitive, pained expression, large dark eyes, and large fleshy ears. It must have been his brother's sincerity and innocence, qualities which femmes fatales seemed to appreciate. Watching her dance before a jukebox blaring Beny More, her ass shaking and body wobbling, her beautiful face the center of attention in that room, Nestor felt triumphant because he knew what the others wished they knew: that yes, her breasts were as round and succulent as they appeared to be under her dress, and that her nipples got big and taut in his lips, and yes, her big rumba ass burned, and yes, the fabulous lips of her vagina parted and sang like the big kiss-me lips of her wide lipsticked mouth, and yes, she had thick black pubic hair, and a mole on the right side of her face and a corresponding mole on the second inner fold of her labia minora; he knew the fine black hair that crept up gradually out the crack of her buttocks, and that when she reached orgasm she would whip her head back and grind her teeth, her body shaking in the aftermath.

Standing by the bar proudly, beside his older brother, Nestor sipped his beer, one bottle after another, until the sea's blueness outside the club windows rustled like a cape and he could shut his eyes and drift like the thick smoke of that room through the crowd of dancers, wrapping himself around the voluptuousness that was Maria.

Two Crimes

Jorge Ibargüengoitia was born in Guanajuato, a small mining town in Central Mexico, and grew up in Mexico City. As the author of plays, novels, and short stories, he won numerous literary awards and saw his work translated into a dozen languages. He also taught Spanish literature at numerous American universities. He was living in Paris at the time of his death in a plane crash in 1987. This is from Two Crimes, *his second novel to be translated into English.*

WHY DID SHE SAY "I LIKE YOU"? I ASKED MYSELF LATER ON WHEN I was in bed. Why, if it is true that she likes me, did she open the door to the patio so the dog could bite me? And why did she say "I like you" afterwards? Another question: Why did she kiss me this morning? Did she really feel like kissing me or was it the only thing that occurred to her to do when I nearly caught her red-handed going through my shirt pockets? Furthermore — as I was cogitating there in bed — granted that Lucero may have found herself in such a tight spot this morning that she had no way out but to kiss me; on the other hand, nothing happened this afternoon to force her to say she liked me if she doesn't like me. My deduction was that she does like me and that this morning, even if she had an ulterior motive, she did want to kiss me. However, countering this theory, of course, is the fact that while I was squeezing her in the patio, she opened the door and let the dog out. She is a very contradictory woman.

I was in the room lying on my back in the dark in one of the twins' beds, covered with a sheet that, in the half-light, I could see raised into a pyramid by my erection. What would the Chamuca say if she saw me in this state over a woman with no ideology? To blot out this disapproving image of the Chamuca, I summoned up the memory of the kiss Lucero had given me and the squeeze I gave her.

The church clock struck a quarter after one, I heard the feathered mules, the bathroom door opening and closing, the toilet being flushed, the bathroom door again, and the mules fading away. Why these sounds should have caused me to conceive a very audacious plan, I don't know. I wondered how long it could take for Amalia to fall fast asleep again. Too late, now, to be drumming up conversations that might clarify the point, such as saying to her, for example: "I suffer from insomnia. What kind of a sleeper are you?" Again, I remembered Lucero kissing me and Lucero setting the glasses down on the little table, and my uncle's remark. I got out of bed at a quarter to two.

I don't know where I got the nerve to walk out into the corridor naked in a house as respectable as my uncle Ramón Tarragona's. Not only naked, but with an erection. Luckily, not even the cenzontle saw me, because Zenaida covers his cage with an old towel. The moon was out. I came to Lucero's bedroom door and turned the knob. I never heard a doorknob—and then the door—move more silently. The sound of the blood pounding in my temples, however, was deafening. I closed the door carefully. It took a little while for me to distinguish the outlines of Lucero's body. She was asleep, sprawled on her belly, arms spread, hands on either side of the pillow, facing the other end of the room, taking up almost the whole bed, which was wide. When I bumped into a chair her breathing changed, when I lifted the covers she moved one leg, and when I got into the bed, she woke up.

"Don't get scared," I said very quietly. "It's me, Marcos."

This was the most dangerous moment. If she yelled, I would be in the soup, but she didn't. She didn't even move. I put my hand on her shoulder, she did not push it away, and I began to feel her body. I discovered then that Lucero slept in a cotton T-shirt and panties. Without changing position, without turning around to look at me, she permitted me to slip my hands under her T-shirt, to fondle her breasts, and to press her against my body so that she would feel my erection. I was positive that in a moment or two I would be having Lucero; at the same time, I realized that I had left the condoms in the dresser drawer in the twins' room, but I was so excited and her body seemed so receptive that I decided to proceed. I put my hands inside her panties and touched her pubic hair, pushed my fingers under the elastic band and tried to slip the panties off. Then Lucero shifted position and brought her legs together.

I never did manage to separate them. First I covered the length of her body with kisses until I reached her toes, then I made believe I had lost interest and turned my back on her, and finally I knelt on the bed, placed my hands on her knees, and tried to pry them apart.

We both put forth our best efforts, but she won out. When the struggle was over, the covers were in a pile on the floor, I was panting, and Lucero was in the fetal position, eyes closed, T-shirt and panties in place. I got off the bed, bumped into the chair again, and, as I opened the door, she spoke for the first time. "Good night," she said.

I was on the verge of slamming the door but instead shut it carefully. I went to the bathroom and peed. I realized that to go back to bed in my condition would be unbearable. Consequently another plan came to mind that was even more dangerous than the previous one. Actually, it was hardly a plan, because I was already carrying it out even before it was conceived. Rather, it was an irresistible impulse. I was inside Amalia's room before I realized it. What a different reception that was! As soon as Amalia heard somebody stumbling into the furniture, she turned on the light. She was wearing a very low-cut nightgown that exposed the upper part of her huge breasts, and she had a cloth tied around her head to keep her hairdo from getting mussed; her mules — they actually did have feathers — were beside the bed. She talked a lot but in a whisper. If I remember correctly, she said, "What's going on? . . . What is the matter with you, Marcos? . . . What do you want? . . . Holy Mother of God! . . . Look at the state you're in! . . . You must be crazy! . . . Think of my reputation! . . . Oh, how wonderful! . . ."

She was quiet, fortunately, after that.

Paradiso

Soapbox: If there was any fairness in the world (not just the lit-erary world) José Lezama Lima would be a household name, and everyone would acknowledge Paradiso *to be one of the greatest novels of the twentieth century. (Just try to find it at your local Barnes & Noble.) It's one of the masterpieces of magic realism. Lezama Lima was a writer's writer in the absolute best sense (and perhaps the only) of the word.*

AFTER FARRALUQUE WAS TEMPORARILY EXILED FROM HIS BUR-lesque throne, José Cemí had an opportunity to witness another phallic ritual. Farraluque's sexual organ was a miniature reproduc-tion of his visage. Even his glans resembled his face. The extension of the frenum looked like his nose, the massive prolongation of the membranous cupola like his bulging forehead. But, among upper-classmen, the phallic power of the rustic Leregas reigned like Aaron's staff. His gladiator's arena was the geography class. He would hide to the left of the teacher on some yellowing benches that held about twelve students. While the class dozed off, listening to an explanation of the Gulf Stream, Leregas would bring out his member — with the same majestic indifference as the key is presented on a cushion in the Velázquez painting—short as a thimble at first, but then, as if driven by a titanic wind, it would grow to the length of the forearm of a manual laborer. Unlike Farraluque's, Leregas's sexual organ did not reproduce his face, but his whole body. In his sexual adventures his phallus did not seem to penetrate but to embrace the other body. Eroticism by compression, like a bear cub squeezing a chestnut, that was how his first moans began.

The teacher was monotonously reciting the text, and most of his pupils, fifty or sixty in all, were seated facing him, but on the left, to take advantage of a niche-like space, there were two benches lined up at right angles to the rest of the class. Leregas was sitting at the end of the first bench. Since the teacher's platform was about a foot high, only the face of this phallic colossus was visible to him. With calm indifference, Leregas would bring out his penis and testicles, and like a wind eddy that turns into a sand column, at touch it became a challenge of exceptional size. His row and the rest of the students peered past the teacher's desk to view that tenacious candle, ready to burst out of its highly polished, blood-filled helmet. The class did not blink and its silence deepened, making the lecturer think that the pupils were morosely following the thread of his discursive expression, a spiritless exercise during which the whole class was attracted by the dry phallic splendor of the bumpkin bear cub. When Leregas's member began to deflate, the coughs began, the nervous laughter, the touching of elbows to free themselves from the stupefaction they had experienced. "If you don't keep still, I'm going to send some students out of the room," the little teacher said, vexed at the sudden change from rapt attention to a progressive swirling uproar.

An adolescent with such a thunderous generative attribute was bound to suffer a frightful fate according to the dictates of the Pythian. The spectators in the classroom noted that in referring to the Gulf's currents the teacher would extend his arm in a curve to caress the algaed coasts, the corals and anemones of the Caribbean. That morning, Leregas's phallic dolmen had gathered those motionless pilgrims around the god Terminus as it revealed its priapic extremes, but there was no mockery or rotting smirk. To enhance his sexual tension, he put two octavo books on his member, and they moved like tortoises shot up by the expansive force of a fumarole. It was the reproduction of a Hindu myth about the origin of the world. The turtle-like books became vertical and one could see the two roes enmeshed in a toucan nest. The roll of dice thrown by the gods out of boredom that morning was to be completely adverse for the vital arrogance of the powerful rustic. The last of the teacher's explanatory syllables resounded like funereal rattles in a ceremony on the island of Cyprus. Leaving at the end of class, the students had the look of people waiting to be disciplined, waiting for the Druid priest to perform the sacrifice. Leregas, foolish-looking, went out with his head tilted to one side. The teacher was somber, like a person petting the dog of a relative who has just died. When they passed, a sudden charge of adrenalin rushed into the teacher's arms; his right hand shot out like a falcon and resounded on Leregas's right cheek, and immediately afterwards his left hand crossed over and found the cocky vitalist's left cheek. Feeling his face transformed into the object of two succulent slaps, Leregas was unabashed; he leaped like a clown, a cynical dancer, a heavy river bird making a triple somersault.

The same absorption that had held the class during the lighting of the country boy's Alexandrian Pharos followed the sudden slaps.

José Lezama Lima

The teacher, with serene dignity, trudged off to the office with his complaints; as he passed, the students were imagining the lecturer's embarrassment in explaining the strange event. Leregas plodded on, not looking around, and got to the study hall with his tongue hanging out. His tongue was a lively poodle pink. Now it was possible to compare the tegument of his glans with that of his oral cavity. Both were a violet pink, but the color of the glans was dry, polished, ready to resist the porous dilation of the moment of erection, while that of the mouth was brighter in tone, shining with the light saliva, as the ebbing tide penetrates a snail on the shore. He used his clownishness to defend himself from the finale of the priapic ceremony somewhat coyly, with some indifference and indolence, as if he had been rewarded for the exceptional importance of his act. He had not meant it to be a challenge, he simply had not made the slightest effort to avoid it. The class, in the second quarter of the morning, was passing through a period conducive to the thickening of galloping adolescent blood, assembled before the essential nothingness of nodding didacticism. Leregas's mouth was receptive, purely passive, and there saliva took the place of maternal water. The mouth and the glans seemed to be at opposite poles, and Leregas's clownish indifference allied him with the hidden femininity of his mouth's liquid pink. His arched eros collapsed completely under the pedagogical slaps. He remembered that the phalli of Egyptian colossi or the giant children spawned by the sons of heaven and the daughters of man did not correspond to their large size, but instead, as in Michelangelo's painted sex in the Creation, the hidden glans hinted at its diminutive dome. Almost all the spectators remembered the arching temerity of that summer morning, but Cemí remembered better the wild provincial's

110

mouth, inside which a small octopus seemed to be stretching, disappearing into the cheeks like smoke, sliding down the channel of the tongue, falling to pieces on the ground like an ice flower with streaks of blood.

Leregas was expelled from school, but Farraluque, who had been condemned to forfeit three Sunday passes, provoked a prolonged sexual chain that touched on the prodigious. The first Sunday of his confinement he wandered through the silent playgrounds and the completely empty study hall. The passage of time became arduous and slow. Time had become a succession of too moist grains of sand inside an hourglass. Creamy, dripping, interminable whipped cream. He tried to abolish time with sleep, but time and sleep retreated until at last they touched backs as during the first moments of a duel, then pacing off the number of steps agreed upon, but no shots rang out. And the prolonged smell of Sunday silence, the silent gun cotton that formed quick clouds, phantasmal chariots with a decapitated driver bearing a letter, all fell apart like smoke with each blow of his whip against the fog.

In his boredom Farraluque crossed the courtyard again, just as the headmaster's maidservant, who had an extremely agreeable face, was coming down the stairs. She apparently wanted to contrive an encounter with the chastened scholar. It was she who had observed him from behind the blinds, carrying the droll bit of gossip to the headmaster's wife.

When she passed by him, she said: "How is it that you're the only one who hasn't gone to visit his family this Sunday?"

"I'm being punished," Farraluque answered dryly. "And the worst part is that I don't know why."

"The headmaster and his wife have gone out," the maid replied.

"We're painting the house. If you help us, we'll try to pay you for it."

Without waiting for a reply, she took Farraluque by the hand, walking by his side as they went up the stairs. When they got to the headmaster's apartment he saw that practically everything was covered with paper; the smell of lime, varnish, and turpentine sharpened the evaporations of all those substances, suddenly scandalizing his senses.

In the living room, she let go of Farraluque's hand and with feigned indifference climbed up on a stepladder and began to slide the brush dripping with whitewash along the walls. Farraluque looked around, and on the bed in the first bedroom he could make out the headmaster's cook, a mammee-colored mulatto girl of nineteen puffed years, submerged in an apparently restless serenity of sleep. He pushed on the half-open door. The neat outline of her back stretched down to the opening of her solid buttocks like a deep, dark river between two hills of caressing vegetation. The rhythm of her breathing was dryly anxious; the sweat of summer, deposited in each small opening of her body, gave a bluish gloss to certain areas of her back. The salt glistened in each of those depressions in her body. The reflections of temptation were awakened by the challenging nearness of her body and her own distance in sleep.

Farraluque undressed swiftly and leaped onto the patchwork of delights. Just then the sleeping woman, without stretching, gave a complete turn, offering the normality of her body to the newly arrived male. The unstartled continuity of the mulatto's breathing eliminated the suspicion of pretense. As the large barb of the small-bodied boy penetrated her, it seemed as if she was going to roll over again, but his oscillations did not break the circle of her sleep. Farraluque was at that point in adolescence when, even after copulation, the erection remains beyond its own ends, at times inviting a frenetic masturbation. The immobility of the sleeping woman now began to unnerve him, but then, peeping through the door of the next room, he saw the little Spanish girl who had led him by the hand, also fast asleep. Her body did not have the distension of the mulatto's, in which the melody seemed to be invading muscular memory. Her breasts were hard, like primal clay, her torso was tense as a pine tree, her carnal flower was a fat spider, nourished on the resin of those same pines, tightly wrapped like a sausage. The carnal cylinder of a strong adolescent boy was needed to split the arachnid down the middle. Farraluque had acquired some tricks and soon began to exercise them. The secret touches of the Spanish girl were more obscure and difficult to decipher. Her sex seemed corseted, like a midget bear in a carnival. A bronze gate, Nubian cavalrymen guarded her virginity. Lips for wind instruments, as hard as swords.

When Farraluque jumped onto the feathery spread in the second room, the rotation of the Spanish girl was the opposite of the mulatto's. She offered the plain of her back and her Bay of Naples. With ease, her copper circle surrendered to the rotund attacks of the glans and the full accumulation of its blooded helmet. This was evidence that the Spanish girl took theological care of her virginity, but that she had little concern for the maidenhood of the remaining parts of her body. The easy flow of blood during adolescence made possible a prodigy which, once normal conjugation was over, enabled him to begin another, *per angustam viam.* This new amorous encounter recalled the incorporation of a dead serpent by its hissing female conqueror. Coil after coil, the momentarily flaccid member was penetrating the body of the conquering serpent, like a monstrous organism of Cenozoic times, in which digestion and reproduction formed a single function. How frequently the marine serpent had come to the grotto of the Spanish girl was apparent from the relaxation of the tunnel, and Farraluque's phallic configuration was extremely propitious for that retrospective penetration, for his barb had an exaggerated length beyond the bearded root. With an astuteness worthy of a Pyrenean ferret, the Spanish girl divided its length into three segments, motivating, more than pauses in her sleep, the true hard breathing of proud victory. The first segment comprised the hardened helmet of the glans and a tense, wrinkled part that extended from the rim of the glans like a string waiting to be plucked. The second segment brought up the strut or, speaking more properly, the stem, the part most involved, for it would give the signal for continuing or abandoning the incorporation. But the Spanish girl, with the tenacity of a classical potter opening the broad mouth of an amphora with only two fingers, managed to unite the two small fibers of the opposing parts and reconcile them in that darkness. She turned her face and told the boy something that at first he did not understand but later on made him smile with pride. The vital luxury of Spanish women often leads them to use a number of Cuban expressions outside of their ordinary meaning, and the attacker on two established fronts heard her exhale pleadingly out of the vehemence of her ecstasy the phrase "permanent wave." This had nothing to do with barbershop dialectics. In asking, she meant for the conductor of energy to beat with the flat of his hand on the foundation of the injected phallus. With each of those blows her ecstasy was transformed into corporeal waves. A tingle in her bones was enlivened by the blow, with the fluency of muscles impregnated by a stellar Eros. The phrase had come to the Spanish girl as something obscure, but her senses had given her an explanation and application as clear as light through a windowpane. Farraluque withdrew his barb, which had worked hard on that day of glory, but the waves continued in the Hispanic squire until her body was slowly carried off in sleep.

◅⟨ SYLVIA LÓPEZ-MEDINA ⟩▻

Cantora

Sylvia Lopez-Medina lives in Santa Cruz, California. This brief but note-perfect shower scene comes from Cantora, *her saga of four generations of Mexican (and Mexican-American) women in Southern California. Based on the oral history of the author's family, the novel proves her to be a strong addition to the chorus of smart women currently reconstructing (reconfiguring?) their own histories.*

FRESH FROM HER BATH AND WRAPPED IN A CLEAN BATHROBE, HAIR dripping, Amparo looked throughout the house for John. Searching the east wing, she heard water running and followed the sound. She entered the spare bedroom and realized this was where John had been sleeping. The bathroom door was ajar. Amparo slowly approached it as she continued drying her hair with a towel. Pressing her fingers against the door, she called out softly.

"John? Are you in here?"

There was no answer. She pushed the door open slightly.

"John?"

She heard what sounded like sobbing. The bathroom was filled with steam. As she entered, the sobbing grew louder. He was standing behind the opaque shower door, his hands on the wall opposite the shower spray. The water was pouring on his back and he appeared to be holding himself up, leaning on the wall and crying.

Amparo watched him for a moment, then she walked across the room towards the shower. John did not hear her. She dropped her towel and took off her terry robe. Gently, she opened the shower door and entered the large tiled stall. Her back against the tile wall, she worked herself between John's arms, and up until she was facing him. Putting her arms around his neck, she began whispering in his ear, but he could not hear her. He opened his eyes and looked at her, amazed, as the water ran like a small river over their bodies. He pulled her to him and buried his face in her hair. As she began kissing him, his sobs transferred to her until they were crying together. He reached behind him and turned off the water, then he lowered her to the tile floor.

Twilight at the Equator

Jaime Manrique was born in Barranquilla, Colombia, and moved to New York when he was seventeen. He has published poetry, short stories, film criticism, and two novels. Although he is probably best known for Latin Moon Over Manhattan *(great title), I've chosen a passage from* Twilight by the Equator, *which I think is an even better book, at once funnier and sadder than its predecessor.*

I WAS SIPPING MY DRINK, WHEN HUMBERTO, LIT UP, RETURNED TO the table—his eyes blazed from the cocaine. When a new song was played, he took to the dance floor. Although he danced like the other men, he made it clear—by giving me furtive glances—that he was dancing for me. Now that I could inspect him, I saw how beautiful he was: he had long sensual limbs, and his tight jeans revealed a nice crotch and a shapely ass. He twirled, with feline movements, an invitation to pleasures rare and exquisite. In his gestures there was the promise of total surrender. I was entranced watching him, getting aroused, when Ramón returned to the table.

"I feel like a new woman," Ramón said. "Makeup and drugs . . . and men, that's all I need to be happy." He noticed Humberto on the dance floor. "Uhm, just what I thought. He likes you. You can do with him whatever you want, darling."

"Is he a hustler?"

"No, Santiago, he's a *chico bien*, a boy from a good family, a sophisticointellectual. He's impressed with you because you're a cosmopolitan writer living in New York. Tonight he'll do anything you want. Absolutely free. Compliments of the house."

"I'm horny for him," I admitted. "But I can't take him to my relatives' house."

"Darling," Ramón snorted. "This isn't New York by any means, but here we have divine decadence, pleasures that the Emperors of China never had. As part of the Friday Night Special we have access to a room equipped with everything: condoms for all sizes and tastes, lubricants, whips, chains, torture instruments, whatever you're into. That's why I put up with everything else I hate about this country—because of the divine decadent pleasures."

It was past midnight when Ramón found someone he liked, and they disappeared into one of the cubicles off the dance floor. Left alone with Humberto, we began to talk about more intimate subjects. Humberto was a literature student at Barranquilla's private university. He had already published short stories and essays in Colombian newspapers, and he was working on his first novel. In this respect, he was no different from many of my students in New York who wanted to be writers. Then he told me about his lover, Raúl, who had died of AIDS just last year. Raúl was an older architect, and they had moved in together, which in Barranquilla amounted to a scandal. Humberto's family had cut him off. They had lived together for a short while, and suddenly Raúl developed AIDS pneumonia and died within a year. As he told me this story, he became human to me. He was more than just a handsome young man—he became a person of depth, someone whose life had been touched by suffering. Moved by his story, I reached over and grabbed his chin. Humberto closed his eyes, and grabbed my hand, squeezing it. The contact of his skin on mine gave me a hard-on. This was no different from going into a bar in Greenwich Village, chatting with a guy, asking him home. Right from the beginning you knew what the outcome would be: you'd have sex, and then you'd get up, exchange phone numbers, and you'd never call each other. I knew that in a few days I would be returning to New York, that Humberto would stay in Barranquilla where his life was, that whatever happened between us would probably have a longer life as a memory. Bluntly, I asked, "Would you like to have sex with me?"

"Yes, I'm attracted to you," he said, taking my hand and nibbling the tip of my fingers.

What happened in bed was a total surprise to me. Perhaps because we both had lost the men we loved to AIDS, perhaps because we had lost them recently, perhaps because we both came from the same culture and had experienced the isolation of a homosexual in a place that denied our existence, perhaps because the tropical night was splendorous and scented with the sweetness of honeysuckle, perhaps because the night seemed to exist just for the purpose of making love, we surrendered to each other with a passion and a totality that I had never experienced before, not even with Ryan. When we kissed, desperately, avidly, it was if we were trying to pass back and forth all the secrets in our souls. When I took his cock in my hand, I held it with wonder, for all its perfection, for all its power to give pleasure, to make me forget—for that miraculous instant — all the sadness and pain of life. We made love on the floor, standing up, on the bed, sitting up, biting, squeezing, pumping, fisting, as if this was the last chance to do with one person everything we had learned about the pleasures of the body. After climaxing, we were embracing when I noticed that he was crying with the same ardor he had made love to me. Shaken by the depth of the feelings I had experienced with this stranger, grateful to be alive, grateful to have experienced an ecstasy that had made me appreciate again what a holy instrument the flesh is, I embraced him with all my strength, and cried, too, until we both did it in unison, as if we were part of a chorus, wailing for everything we had loved and lost.

◄ GABRIEL GARCÍA MÁRQUEZ ►

Love in the Time of Cholera

Gabriel García Márquez may be our greatest living writer. (Whether you rank him number two, number three, or number eight hardly matters.) More than any other single book, One Hundred Years of Solitude *was the catalyst responsible for the worldwide recognition of Latin American fiction. I've chosen an excerpt not from that masterpiece but from* Love in the Time of Cholera, *my personal favorite among his works.*

AUSENCIA SANTANDER WAS ALMOST FIFTY YEARS OLD AND LOOKED it, but she had such a personal instinct for love that no homegrown or scientific theories could interfere with it. Florentino Ariza knew from the ship's itineraries when he could visit her, and he always went unannounced, whenever he wanted to, at any hour of the day or night, and never once was she not waiting for him. She would open the door as her mother had raised her until she was seven years old: stark naked, with an organdy ribbon in her hair. She would not let him take another step until she had undressed him, because she thought it was bad luck to have a clothed man in the house. This was the cause of constant discord with Captain Rosendo de la Rosa, because he had the superstitious belief that smoking naked brought bad luck, and at times he preferred to put off love rather than put out his inevitable Cuban cigar. On the other hand, Florentino Ariza was very taken with the charms of nudity, and she removed his clothes with sure delight as soon as she closed the door, not even giving him time to greet her, or to take off his hat or his glasses, kissing him and letting him kiss her with sharp-toothed kisses, unfastening his clothes from bottom to top, first the buttons of his fly, one by one after each kiss, then his belt buckle, and at the last his vest and shirt, until he was like a live fish that had been slit open from head to tail. Then she sat him in the living room and took off his boots, pulled on his trouser cuffs so that she could take off his pants while she removed his long underwear and at last she undid the garters around his calves and took off his socks. Then Florentino Ariza stopped kissing her and letting her kiss him so that he could do the only thing he was responsible for in that precise ceremony: he took his watch and chain out of the button-hole in his vest and took off his glasses and put them in his boots so he would be sure not to forget them. He always took that precaution, always without fail, whenever he undressed in someone else's house.

As soon as he had done that, she attacked him without giving him time for anything else, there on the same sofa where she had just undressed him, and only on rare occasions in the bed. She mounted him and took control of all of him for all of her, absorbed in herself, her eyes closed, gauging the situation in her absolute inner darkness, advancing here, retreating there, correcting her invisible route, trying another, more intense path, another means of proceeding without drowning in the slimy marsh that flowed from her womb, droning like a horsefly as she asked herself questions and answered in her native jargon; where was that something in the shadows that only she knew about and that she longed for just for herself, until she succumbed without waiting for anybody, she fell alone into her abyss with a jubilant explosion of total victory that made the world tremble. Florentino Ariza was left exhausted, incomplete, floating in a puddle of their perspiration, but with the impression of being no more than an instrument of pleasure. He would say: "You treat me as if I were just anybody." She would roar with the laughter of a free female and say: "Not at all: as if you were nobody." He was left with the impression that she took away everything with mean-spirited greed, and his pride would rebel and he would leave the house determined never to return. But then he would wake for no reason in the middle of the night, and the memory of the self-absorbed love of Ausencia Santander was revealed to him for what it was: a pitfall of happiness that he despised and desired at the same time, but from which it was impossible to escape.

❈ ENRIQUE MEDINA ❈

Las Tumbas (The Tombs)

Since it was first published in 1972, Enrique Medina's Las Tumbas (The Tombs), *a tough, original, totally uncompromising story of adolescence in a reform school, has been a* cause célèbre *of contemporary Argentine fiction. It was banned by the military junta that ruled from 1975 to 1983. When it was returned to print in 1984, it was in its thirtieth edition. In addition, Medina has written other novels, short stories, essays, chronicles, and children's books and remains a vigorous and steadfastly contestorial figure in Argentine literature.*

MISSY GABRIELA IS REALLY THE ONE WHO TAUGHT ME HOW TO make the ones who misbehave see the light. Of course, I know how. But since she has a little jerk by the hand, it's no problem for her to show me all over again.

The kid is fierce and won't give in. But he does, oh god, how he does! Shit runs down the little jerk's legs. Missy Gabriela gets so carried away with herself that she gets her white coat dirty when she comes up to him from behind. I don't miss the chance to call her attention to it.

She's shouting at the kid like she's crazy. She grabs him by the

127

hair and shoves him into the dormitory and then drags him to the bathroom. It's just like an adventure film. Second installment. Missy Gabriela lets him catch his breath while she takes her jacket off. She hands it to me to put on the bed for her.

She goes at it again and the kid closes his eyes again. Maybe it's a game or maybe he has a tic. Missy Gabriela corners him and makes his ears ring. Every so often you find out something new. Missy Gabriela puts her knee into the small of the kid's back. I wasn't aware of that trick. The knee trick has two functions. First, to take over when your fist gets worn out. Second, to press into the kid's back while you pull his arms back.

The two functions seem to work great and the jerk looks about ready to croak with each new attack. Missy Gabriela prefers the second job for the knee. Well, there's no accounting for tastes. She leans against the wall, and with one hand she grabs the kid's two arms from behind, using the tips of her shoes to work his legs over.

She pulls the kid's hair so hard that his head digs into her tits. She's really in a rage. The kid is crying, with blood and snot all over the place. She pulls his hair down slowly and the kid's face stretches like it was made of rubber. She makes his head touch his back, and his pants slip down a bit, his shirt inches up and you can see his belly heaving up and down.

Missy Gabriela twists her mouth like she's trying to work up a maternal smile. She's got cute teeth and her lipstick is smeared a little. She shakes the kid's head and asks him softly, her smile playing around her face, if he's going to keep on acting up.

Of course the kid doesn't understand a shit of what she says. He probably thinks it's his guardian angel talking to him. Missy Gabriela then moves on to a well-known technique, digging her fingernails into the guy's lower lip.

The kid is down between her knees and can't kick. Missy Gabriela is still propped up against the wall. The kid looks up, and Missy Gabriela looks down. His face is covered with blood. Missy Gabriela yanks down on his hair. If she keeps on this way she'll end up with his head down to his ass. But she lets up, and the head goes back to her tits.

Third episode. The knot of Missy Gabriela's hair has come loose and I'm fascinated. It really turns me on although why the hell it should is beyond me. She's ugly but one day when I went into the bathroom, I found her drying her hair after washing it, and I discovered that her hair, which fell forward from her head, came all the way down to her pussy. She stuck her hand in her hair to part it so she could see me, and she smiled at me. I scrammed fast, all nerves and with my body like someone was tickling me.

The little creep's head was bobbing up and down between her tits. Her knot was coming more and more undone and I couldn't take my eyes off it. The pressure of her fingernail on his lower lip must have been terrible because the kid snapped to and tried to get away. I caught him just in time and bounced him back to Missy Gabriela. She smiled at me, and I smiled back.

I kept my eye on the knot that kept getting looser and looser. She grabbed him by the neck and jammed her tits into his head. They both were breathing hard. Missy Gabriela started to calm him down and I started to get worried, her knot needed just a few more minutes to work itself completely loose.

She wiped the sweat off her face with her hand and discovered that her hair was falling down to her shoulders. Luckily, the kid moved! Missy Gabriela shook him again for all she was worth. I ran to pick her hairpins up from the floor and held them for dear life. Her hair now fell all over the jerk's chest. That ought to be my chest, you little fucker. Her hair danced around with each blow. Then she threw him under the shower.

The water flooded over his face. It fell onto his shirt streaked with blood and onto his pants, his legs, his shoes, washing away in a thousand colors on the tiles. So much water to hide such a little piece of shit.

"You little turd! Strip down and wash yourself good! And don't get out until I say to!"

I knew the kid wouldn't budge even if the world came to an end. The water would bring him back to life, the more water the better. Missy Gabriela crossed to the other side of the room and started to breathe deep and regular.

Fourth episode. She pulled her hair back.

"Do you see how you've got to handle these creeps?"

"Yes, Missy Gabriela."

"What are you gawking at?"

She smiled at me. She went over to the wash basin and soaped her arms. She shook her head.

"You're great, Missy Gabriela."

She lifted her hair up and looked at me. She smiled and I smiled back. She lowered her hand and her hair fell open like a fan. Like an unending waterfall.

"Your hair is very pretty, Missy Gabriela." She lifted her hair again to look at me.

"You like it?"

"Yes, Missy Gabriela."

"Hand me the towel."

I handed it to her and she dried herself off. The hair under her arms was pretty.

"Tell that shithead not to move from the shower until I tell him he can."

I do what she tells me to.

"Would you like to comb it for me?"

"Yes, Missy Gabriela."

She sits down on a white bench with her back toward me and hands me a large comb over her shoulder. When I take it, my hand touches hers. Slowly I run the comb down her back toward her hips. She throws her head back and closes her eyes.

"You like it?"

"Yes, Missy Gabriela."

I want to tell her she's great but I start to stutter. She lets her head fall all the way back and her hair bunches up on my shirt. We're in the same position as when she had a hold of the little jerk. Except now she's the jerk and I'm her.

"What are you saying?"

"How good you are to me."

She laughs and straightens her head up. I continue combing her. I can't stand it anymore. I grab her hair with both hands and rub my face with it. She stands up and slaps me in the face. I grab on to her. With her arm on my throat she makes an effort to shove me away. Silence is witness to my greater strength. She takes her arm away and holds my head against her chest. She leans over me. She lifts her arm, her hand on my neck. She covers me, wrapping me completely in her hair.

◈| ALVARO MUTIS |◈

"The Tramp Steamer's Last Port of Call" *in* The Adventures of Maqroll: Four Novellas

Alvaro Mutis was born in Bogota, Colombia, spent his childhood in Brussels, and currently lives in Mexico. He is the author of poetry, short stories, and novels. He has won many literary awards. Gabriel García Márquez: "Mutis is one of the greatest writers of our time." No argument here. This excerpt of "The Tramp Steamer's Last Port of Call" is from perhaps his best work, The Adventures of Maqroll: Four Novellas.

THERE WAS NO MESSAGE FOR HIM. HE MET WITH SOME CLIENTS TO arrange a shipment of olive oil and fine wines to Helsinki. Autumn was slipping away, and Lisbon showed the opaque, melancholy face so attuned to the fados that tourists pretend to enjoy in the taverns. He returned to the ship with an overwhelming exhaustion grinding inside him like the beginning of a tropical disease. He had lost all interest in the *Halcyon*, and when he saw the tramp steamer lying at anchor in the middle of the bay as it waited for a berth at the docks, its graceless figure awakened in him a combination of irritation and apathy. As he was about to climb down to the launch that would take him out to the freighter, he heard a woman's voice calling from a distance: "Jon! Jon! Wait for me." Warda was running along the street that led down to the waterfront. She wore cream-colored slacks and a red blouse, and waved a light-beige sweater to attract his attention. He stood, not moving, on the dock, while an uncontrollable joy exploded in the middle of his chest. When Warda reached his side she kissed him on the cheek; he could barely respond with a light brush against the slightly moist skin of the face that had obsessed him for so long. Without saying a word, she put her arm through his and led him toward the center of the city. They crossed the Avenida Vinte e Quatro de Julho and walked along the Rua do Alecrim. She said that surely some bar would be open in the narrow streets of the Bairro Alto. "I thought you weren't coming. I imagined you on your way to the Orthodox holy places." "For now there's another orthodoxy that has to be taken care of," she replied with a meaningful glance, amused at the expression that must have been on Jon's face. Iturri had that intrinsic Basque inability to hide his emotions. "We found a bar, and there we revealed our feelings, slowly but implacably. I admitted that if she hadn't come I would have gone to Australia to work on a coastal trader," Jon said in a voice that after so many years still betrayed an unexpected despair completely foreign to his upright, reserved character. He recalled very little of their conversation. Warda, without losing the serenity and balance that lent so much charm to her youth, confessed that her presumptive European education had been an unmitigated disaster and that all she cared about now was to be with him. Something in him filled her with a plenitude she had never known before. It was all she wanted. She did not believe the future offered any chance for them to build a life together. She didn't care about that either. What she needed now, needed like the air she breathed, was to live fully in the present. Jon stammered something about the difference in their ages, their nationalities, their customs. Warda shrugged and with the certainty of a clairvoyant replied that he didn't believe a word he was saying and none of it mattered in the least. It was six in the evening and they had consumed several bottles of vinho verde along with some perfectly unmemorable fried fish. They went to her hotel on the Avenida da Liberdade and tried to walk in with firm, natural steps. Jon registered as Warda's husband, and they rode up to the room in an embrace so close that the elevator operator turned around a few times to see if they were still breathing. Every article of clothing they were wearing lay scattered on the floor between the door and the bed.

"We made love again and again, with the slow, meticulous intensity of people who don't know what will happen tomorrow. Warda's obsessive desire to fill the present with meaning was based on her intelligent and accurate assessment of the limited possibilities and hopeless obstacles our relationship offered. As I had said in the bar, I couldn't see where it would lead either. And so, with a surrender that bordered on desperation, we took refuge in the pleasure of our bodies. Warda, when she was naked, acquired a kind of aura that emanated from the perfection of her body, the texture of her moist, elastic skin, and that face: Seen from above, when we were in bed, it took on even more of the qualities of a Delphic vision. It's not easy to explain or describe. Sometimes I think it never happened. The only thing that has stopped me when

I've wanted to die is the thought that this image would die with me." When he reached these barriers to communicating his experience, Iturri would fall into long silences in which profound despair stirred up its bitter dregs. Then he went on. "We spent three days in the Hotel de Lisboa and never left the room. We had turned it into a kind of private universe, a slow alternation between almost wordless lovemaking and an exchange of confidences about our childhoods and our discovery of the world. Warda possessed a very peculiar idea of a sailor's life. I had little to tell her about my own experience at sea. Nothing unusual had happened to me in a profession filled with gray tedium relieved only by the changes in climate and landscape that constant travel necessarily imposes. I can't reconstruct our conversations now. I do remember that her character made them serene and full, and that anecdotes and surprises gave way to the examination and assimilation of our personal visions of the world and its people. As I've said, Warda had something of the sibyl about her. She moved through the half-trance of her sensations with the confidence of a sleepwalker. In this she was as fully Oriental as any genie in the *Arabian Nights*."

◅ LOIDA MARITZA PÉREZ ▻

Geographies of Home

Loida Maritza Pérez is from the Dominican Republic. Her first novel, Geographies of Home, *has been called "stunning," "original," "haunting," and "powerful." It provides the shortest excerpt in the book, barely over two hundred words, but it's a perfectly realized scene and one that's quintessentially Latin.*

SILENTLY, STEALTHILY, SHE'D SLIP INTO HIS ROOM TO JOIN HIM IN his bed. From between her naked breasts she would magically produce a mango whose green skin fading into pink hinted at the ripe perfection of the fruit inside. Her fingers would gently knead the fruit, transforming its pulp into a nectar that moved tantalizingly beneath its skin. Then, lips scarcely opening, she'd puncture the mango's tip. The bit of flesh her teeth had torn would drift onto her lap. Her lips would bloom into a bud against the fruit's small wound, and her hands would massage its flesh, cajoling its nectar into her mouth. Any drops that rolled onto her chin she'd offer to Papito on a fingertip. Hungrily, shamelessly, he would lick them off. Only when he had begged for more would she recklessly strip off the mango's skin and offer the fruit to him in the hollow of her palm. Rivulets of its juice would ooze onto her fingers. Papito would reach his tongue between them. One by one he would take her fingers into his mouth and lingeringly suck each. When unable to postpone any longer savoring the fruit itself against his lips and tongue and teeth, he would twine his hands through his love's dark hair and draw her near so that she too might partake.

◖ CECILE PINEDA ◗

The Love Queen
of the Amazon

For over a dozen years Cecile Pineda produced experimental the-
ater pieces with her own ensemble company before turning her
considerable talents to fiction. She has written four novels (and
is the single most pleasant author with which I have had corre-
spondence), including The Love Queen of the Amazon, *from which*
the following is taken.

ANA MAGDALENA HAD NEVER LIKED DANDELION SALAD. SHE FOUND
it too tough and too bitter for her delicate and discriminating palate. It was not meant for human consumption, particularly not for
humans who were troubled. Even in normal times, she believed
dandelions were for cattle to graze on, to bring up repeatedly from
one stomach or other. She picked over leaf after leaf. Over and
over Aurora Constancia's advice haunted her: *You don't have to like*
him just because you're married to him. Just go through the motions.
After you're married, things get more interesting. You'll have money
to spend, a carriage. . . . And all the time she could see the muscles
of Sergio Ballado writhing under his glistening, sunburned skin.
She remembered the sound of her own voice. It was a new sound,

139

one with which she had only now become acquainted. *It's my virginity, and I'll present proof of it as I please. And to whom I please.*

By the time Ana Magdalena rose from the table, her dandelions had hardly been touched, but a new and shining resolve had come to visit her restive heart. She retired to her room for the siesta and carefully shut the door. Bracing a chair against the knob, she set about shedding her clothes. Off came the pinafore and the oppressively plain brown frock, off came the cotton chemise, down came the slip and the drawers with their demure lace cuffs. Ana Magdalena stood coolly surveying herself before the massive antique mirror of the armoire. She placed her hands beneath the small white doves of her breasts. She raised them ever so slightly toward the glass. At once, her nipples sprang to life. They stood proud, like fat, rosy little beaks eagerly testing the air. She passed her hands over the rounding contours of her belly. She raised her arms to exult in the dense tufts of thick black hair that marked her body's secret hollows. Slowly she turned her back, craning her neck to survey the high and blushing rotundities of her cheeks, and to admire the two provocative dimples that nestled at the base of her spine.

Ana Magdalena had never really examined herself naked. It was a new sensation, one that required no effort to get used to, but it left her breathless and slightly dizzy. Yet she knew there was little time just now for any dreamy self-indulgence. She flung open the armoire and retrieved a silk chemise, which she quickly threw over her head. She found a matching pair of lacy silk drawers of a semi-transparency that betrayed the contours of her loveliness to shadowy advantage. Over these she raised the wine-dark silk velvet dress, the one she had worn to Aurora Constancia's wedding. It was a dress cut on the bias so cunningly that it molded itself to every sinew, every curve. She closed the armoire once again. She turned slowly to gauge the effect. She was not displeased. In a small beaded purse, she stuffed only the barest essentials: a handkerchief and a mirror. She picked up a pair of high-heeled slippers. She was ready. Carefully she opened the window casement. She stood on a chair to ease herself over the sill and quietly let herself down into the flower bed below. She brushed the dirt from her bare feet, and slipped into the shoes.

❧ ELENA PONIATOWSKA ❧

Tinisima

Though Elena Poniatowska was born in Paris, she went on to become one of Mexico's leading literary and intellectual figures. She was a prolific writer, a journalist, essayist, and novelist, consistently producing work of extremely high quality. This is from her novel Tinisima, *based on the life of Tina Modosti.*

JULIO IS NO LONGER BY HER SIDE TO CALM HER DOWN, REASSURE her. She faces the storm; she faces the storm alone. And the future? What would have happened? Would there have been a place for Tina? Julio said they would live together on the island, and Tina was prepared to share his fate. Once that tropical Mussolini was defeated, Julio would build a new socialist Cuba along the lines of the Russian Revolution. He would form a Central American and Caribbean anti-imperialist league, break relations with the United States, offer the peasants education, medicine, and decent food. Cubans would learn to produce for their own needs, they would develop their own science and technology. They would even make cameras. Yes, Tina, you will make films in the streets of Havana, surrounded by your students, films for the people and by the people; you'll see, my love, what a country my country is, we will make love morning, noon, and night, the arts will blossom like the large red flowers of the royal poinciana tree, the petals of your lips will burn at the hour of love, our island is guided by the light in a woman's eyes; Cuba needs your eyes, as I need your saliva, the tears from your eyes.

Exhausted, drenched in a cold sweat, she tosses and turns in bed, a moan of pain accompanying each movement. Is she the only one who has been left with these images of love? Are there others he loved the same way? He is the only one she has loved with such yearning, such passions, such a willingness to be completely open. Often, after they went their separate ways, Tina would sit down on a bench in the Ciudadela before going to work. She loved him so intensely that getting away from him for moments was her only salvation. Memories of last night's lovemaking played havoc with her senses. She began to shiver: her lips would remember his smile of satisfaction, the hair falling over his forehead, the weight of his legs, his hands on her back, her neck, her belly. She could almost feel his mouth on hers, Julio on top of her, yes, Julio, convulsing, exploding in spasms; yes, Julito, yes. She would pull herself together as she went over each moment one by one. She had loved Weston, her teacher, but never with such urgency, such a compelling ache.

Half an hour later, Tina would get up from the park bench and somehow or other make her way to 54 Mesones. Maybe he'll finish early today and come pick me up. Once inside the office, she would jump each time the door opened. I hear Julio's steps. It is Julio. No, it isn't. When will he come? My heart aches; I can't live like this. It is late. What happened to him? What's happening to me? I'm being consumed by love. I don't think I'll be able to work, she repeated to herself. The attraction between them was so fierce that when he finally entered the office she would feel the beating of her pulse in her belly. I'm crazy: to desire a man like this is madness. I am feverish; each day is a new delirium. I used to be a normal woman, and now I can't do anything but wait for him.

She didn't understand anything except Julio's gestures, Julio's hands on her body.

Sometimes they made love as if it were a game. The bed, the sheets, the blankets, everything spun around them, as light and playful as feathers. Sometimes Julio would arrive home in a serious mood; then, neither the blankets nor anything else would dance. There was something desperate in the way he would bury himself in her. One night Tina was awakened by his sobs; she took him in her arms and sheltered his head between her breasts until their desire returned. Mella clung to her like a drowning man, pulling her down, her name coming in one long sigh: Tina, Tina, Tina, Tinaaaa. Again, the tears on her shoulder. For the sake of modesty, she didn't turn on the light or look at him. She felt his sobs and let them come as she caressed him softly, softly, softly.

The next morning a warm yellow light crept over their bed, their feet, their knees. When it reached their bellies, Julio awoke. He was no longer the same man as the night before. He woke up to the world, the sun, the transparency of the air. Day came to greet him and again they made love, laughing, pressed to each other, their legs white with semen, musk, sandalwood, their skins shining.

It was the quality of light, the way it advanced over the floor and encroached on the whitewashed walls, that grounded their morning lovemaking. This was their way of settling themselves into the day, into life. "We have the same surface area," Julio would say and laugh. "We have the same perimeter, the same mouth." They came together. They became one another. Merged into one. Tied together. Afterwards, at the breakfast table, it was difficult not to share even their bites of food, don't swallow yet, wait for me. When Julio lifted his cup, Tina instantly did the same, just one, you and I, eating from the same plate with the same fork and knife, the same morsels in our mouths. Any other way would have been inconceivable.

The Big Banana

The title of Honduran writer Roberto Quesada's novel The Big
Banana *may be a little joke aimed at the new hometown he's
taken up for the past decade or so: New York (The Big Apple).
It's about Eduardo Lin, a Honduran actor who comes to New York
City and his many (mis)adventures in the city's bohemian Latin
colony. Besides, this is supposed to be a mostly contemporary
anthology, so I thought I should have at least one scene of phone
sex.*

"ALÓ, ALÓ, HELLO, CARIÑO . . ."

"Eduardo . . . I was thinking about you just this second. What a
coincidence!"

"It's not a coincidence, it's astral communication, ultradimen-
sional, telepathic, sort of."

"What's wrong, *amor*, are you becoming a Buddhist?"

"No, I don't think it has anything to do with Buddhism. Besides,
I still haven't met Richard Gere . . . he knows about Buddhism."

"So then, what's it called?"

"What?"

"Whatever it is that's teaching you to take astral trips . . ."

"It's a friend, Casagrande. He believes in those things. I'll explain it to you in a letter."

"Yes, I hope you do. I wrote an article titled 'Bonfire of the Multitudes.' I hope you like it. I love it. I put it in the mail to you today."

"Good, *cariño*, I'll read it as soon as I receive it. This call's going to be brief; when it's over, I have to start cursing at the telephone company."

"Yes, *cariño*. Whenever you say."

"Where are you right now?"

"In my room, *cariño*."

"What are you wearing?"

"I'm in a bathrobe."

"And what else?"

"There you go . . . no."

"Yes, I want to imagine you."

"I'm braless."

"And what else?"

"I'm wearing teeny bikini panties like the ones you like."

"What color?"

"Sky blue."

"Will you take your bathrobe off?"

"No."

"Please . . ."

"No, *cosa*, what's going on?"

"It's love, *mi amor*."

"I'm embarrassed."

"Why?"

"What if the phones are bugged, and someone's listening in?"

"No problem, they can masturbate."

"*Tonto . . .*"

"Will you take it off?"

"Done, I'm in my bikini."

"I'm in my bed, completely naked. I'm hard."

"And now?"

"Now stroke your neck. Run your fingers lightly over your neck. Are you feeling me?"

"Yes, I'm feeling you, do you feel me?"

"Say things to me."

"Like what?"

"Like how we're going to do it when we see each other."

"I'm going to move down to your belly button, I'm going to bite that big thing of yours through your shorts. I'm going to scratch you slowly with my teeth, and when you can't take it any more, I'm going to pull it out and I'm going to eat it."

"What else? I can't take it."

"I have my fingers in between my legs. I'm wet. I'm getting wetter by the second."

"Close your eyes. I'm there beside you. Do you feel my tongue?"

"I feel it."

"Where's your clitoris? I can't find it."

"A little further up.

"Around here?"

"Yes, around there, over to the left."

"Am I doing all right?"

"You're on it. I feel your saliva. I feel your tongue."

"I cut my lower lip with a hair."

"What does it matter, keep going."

"I feel your mouth on my shorts."

"I'm there."

"I'm shorts-less."

"I know, *cariño*, I can feel that thing, it's hard as a tree, like an iron rod. That's how I like it, *cosa*."

"I can't take it."

"Come, *cariño*. On my breasts."

"No, inside."

"No, I might get pregnant. It's better if I turn over."

"Yes."

"I'll get like a kittycat."

"Yeah."

"You like it like this?"

"Yeah."

"Do you want to come? Pull it out and spread it all over my back, on my cheeks, careful not to get it on my hair, I'm too lazy to wash it."

"I love you."

"Me too."

"I want you."

"Me too."

"I'm going."

"Come, *amor*, come."

"I'm . . . oh no, oh Mirian, *mi amor*, I love you."

"Me too . . ."

". . . Thank you NYT."

". . . What? What did you say?"

". . . Thank you New York Telephone!"

She was in bed with the cordless phone, naked, like a kitten, as if she'd just finished making love. He was in his room, exhausted, gurgling into the phone, drawing circles on his belly and chest and writing Mirian on himself again and again with his index finger, like a pencil in the ink-like semen.

Rasero

Francisco Rebolledo was born in Mexico City. For many years he was a chemistry teacher. When he turned to writing, the result was Rasero, *a novel both sensual and cerebral, an intoxicating mix of eighteenth-century politics, desire, philosophy, science, and art. Its protagonist, Fausto Rasero, both intellectually and sexually precocious, is also (and this is Robelledo's master-stroke) orgasmically clairvoyant. At the moment of carnal release he experiences apocalyptic visions of the future, visions the reader recognizes as the horrors of our own century: the Holocaust, the atomic bomb, and so on.*

You HAD RECENTLY SETTLED IN PARIS, VERY HAPPY AT HAVING FI-nally left the court and its horde of schemers. You celebrated the event in your townhouse, drinking plenty of bubbling wine from Champagne, eating crawfish, and frolicking about with your tireless friend, Claudia de Saissac, a warm and generous woman with few equals—with long limbs, large eyes, and an enormous mouth, able to down pleasure whole, in a single gulp. The two of you made love as though your lives depended on it; you pinched each other, bit each other, and went about your licentious coupling with the vigor that can come only from knowing that you are young and eternal. You had, naturally, a number of visions, although you didn't pay them very much attention; the champagne in your head and the avid mouth of Madame de Saissac on your body distracted you from them. What's more, you were tired of those images that had lately been repeating themselves monotonously: soldiers dressed in green, covered with dust, with heavy rifles slung over their shoulders, marching through cities in ruins; the clumsy iron vehicles, advancing slowly and implacably, grinding to pieces any debris that appeared in their path . . . nothing but war and its consequences, as though those phantoms that visited you during orgasm had nothing better with which to be concerned. As dawn broke, the two of you made love for the last time of that night; you thought you couldn't come again, your back hurt, and you felt drier than a grape lying forgotten in the desert sun. But the skillful contortions of your friend, along with the work her tongue did on your ear, managed eventually to make you explode. It was an intense and prolonged orgasm, a fruit ripened by excitement and weariness, that plunged you into a terrifying vision: what you had seen fleetingly just a few days before, those unclear images of Asians being burned to cinders in seconds, repeated itself, but now you had more time to look at the horror. It was a big city alongside the sea; enormous iron ships appeared at the end of streets with people — all of them Asians — hurrying up and down in both directions. Suddenly, the light . . . a light of a greater intensity than any you had seen in your life. It was like peering into the heart of the sun, a blue-white light that reminded you of the one inside the ovens at Sèvres when they reach a heat sufficient to harden the porcelain. But here the light was immense; it covered everything. In an instant — which to you seemed eternal—the terrible intense glow melted every object in its reach. The buildings, the vehicles, and the iron posts along the streets were softened in seconds, as though they were made of wax, and the scorched debris mounted upward with prodigious speed, forming a giant whirlwind. The people—you managed to see only some of them—were incinerated instantly, each in a minuscule flash, like one of the little balls of phosphorus your teacher Ulloa smilingly watched explode in the air when he removed them from the flask of oil that contained them. The light disappeared at once; a dense darkness took its place. That was due to the dust, the earth, the debris, the remains of human beings that overhead, very high up, had formed a great cloud hiding the sun. Madame de Saissac smiled in satisfaction seeing you with your closed eyelids aslant with pleasure. You moved over to one side, embraced her, and pretended to be asleep; your head was full of light and little balls of exploding phosphorus. After a time, your friend, taking care not to awaken you, got out of bed and dressed.

Leopard in the Sun

Laura Restrepo has lived in Colombia, Argentina, Mexico, and Spain. Always actively interested in politics and journalism as well as fiction, she was the political editor of the weekly magazine Semana *while a professor of literature at the National University, Colombia. In 1984, she was a leading member of the peace commission that brought the Colombian government and the guerrillas to the negotiating table. This scene is taken from her 1993 novel,* Leopard in the Sun, *the best book written about the lives of Colombian drug kingpins.*

AT FOUR O'CLOCK IN THE MORNING IN THE CITY'S RED-LIGHT DIStrict a cream-colored Mercedes-Benz 500 SE with tinged bulletproof windows and white calfskin upholstery stops suddenly in front of a black windowless wall, broken only by a neon sign reading "The Blue Siren Topless Bar and Strip Club—Authentic Sirens to Make Your Wildest Dreams Come True." Two Toyotas with armed bodyguards pull up behind the Mercedes.

A huge man limps out of the Mercedes and enters the establishment, peering into the smoke-filled room through black Ray-Ban sunglasses. Nando Barragán pauses a few moments in order to make out the figures dancing in the darkness to the meringue hit "De-vórame Otra Vez." He scans the room with a practiced eye, making a mental picture of it. In all there are twelve available women, scantily dressed: two butterflies, a peacock, two mermaids, a lolli-pop, two transvestites, a rabbit, a tiger, and two plain whores.

"The black Mermaid, the Peacock, and the Tiger," he says to his men, abruptly leaving and going to his car to wait.

"In the old days, before the attempt on his life that damaged his knee, Nando would arrive at The Blue Siren, order the doors locked, and buy drinks all around. Then he'd climb up on the stage to fondle the strippers, stuffing dollar bills in their G-strings, and invariably wind up taking off his own clothes."

"They say his member was ridiculously small, like a tortilla chip in the middle of that colossal body, but that in spite of his lack of attributes, he made women feel good and there was always enough left over for a second round, but they say lots of things, not all of which are true. For example, some say he was completely covered with fine hair, like a monkey, but the truth is that his skin was waxy and hairless, like all yellow-skinned people of the desert."

The bodyguards approach an immense black woman dressed like a mermaid, a blonde with a tail of peacock feathers, and a skinny girl with striped ears and a tail wearing an imitation tiger-skin body-suit. They say something to the three women, who hur-riedly cover themselves, grab their bags, and run out to the street, balancing on six-inch spike heels, pushing each other like high school girls.

The women climb into the Mercedes in a jumble of squeals and scrambling, the Peacock in front and the Mermaid and the Tiger in back. But Nando doesn't approve and rearranges things so that the Mermaid ends up in front with him and the Tiger and the Peacock are in back. The Mercedes and the Toyotas take off through the streets, tires burning and screeching. Once they are under way, the Peacock decides to open the door and in a sharp curve almost falls out of the car, but she's saved when someone grabs a plume and pulls her back in. Farther down the road they stop in front of a mariachi plaza, and at Nando's signal the bodyguards gather a trusted trio and put them in one of the Toyotas.

The caravan heads down the coast, taking a mountain road along the shoreline. The sea pounds against the rocky cliffs. The tremendous, roaring waves are black, green, and violet. Nando is steering the car at sixty miles per hour with one hand and holding a whiskey bottle in the other. He alternates gulps of whiskey with drags from the Pielroja cigarettes the women stick in his mouth. Flying low, drunk, ignoring the force of gravity beckoning him at each curve in the road, Nando fires his Colt at the signs warning of danger ahead.

The girls are exhilarated. Swept up by the car's speed and the party atmosphere, they have given themselves over to the booze and smoke and busy themselves with pleasing their host. While one kisses him another gives him a blow job and the third whispers love sonnets in his ear. They pour Old Parr down his throat and throw the empty bottles out the windows to see the brown glass shatter against the asphalt in a thousand golden stars and laugh as the Toyotas swerve to avoid the shards.

At Nando's request, the Mermaid starts a fierce striptease while she murmurs a meringue with the hoarse voice of a ruined Indian. She unfastens a bra festooned with metal scales like medieval armor, and two monumental tits, worthy of *The Guinness Book of*

World Records, burst free, nipples firmly planted in the center of each like a cyclops's eye. Each of the Mermaid's breasts is huge and black, real heavyweight champions. On the left is Frazier and on the right, Muhammad Ali, duking it out with the bouncing and rolling of the car on the road. A turn to the left and Frazier falls on Ali, pushing him onto the ropes. A turn to the right and Ali comes back with an uppercut to Frazier's jaw. In the excitement of the scuffle, the nipples harden and open like satellite disks sending pornographic messages of war.

The passengers in the front seat are packed in like sardines in a tin, as if instead of two oversized people there were four, Nando the Gorilla, the Mermaid, better known as the Whale, the huge breast Frazier, and his twin brother, Ali.

The Mermaid takes off her tailfin of wire and silver lame, freeing the wild nest between her legs. Her sex is overwhelming and prodigious like a vortex, emitting animal fluids that further excite Nando. He pushes a bottle into the meaty Amazon cave until it disappears from sight, completely devoured, the old man with the beard on the label lost from sight.

"You tricked me, Mermaid," cries Nando, disenchanted. "Mermaids aren't supposed to have a hole even the size of the eye of a needle, but you have a canyon that if I entered, I could see your tonsils."

In the backseat, the Peacock, a blonde with long hair, has fallen asleep with her mouth and eyes open. Nando orders the Tiger to wake her up and pluck her feathers. The Tiger, who is skinny but vicious, slaps the Peacock, then shakes and bites her, but the Peacock remains mute and absent, lost in who knows what alcohol-induced purgatory. Next, the Tiger, angry and unwilling to accept failure, scratches the Peacock with her sharp nails, yanks feathers from her tail, and pulls her hair, which falls to the floor revealing a shaved head, smooth as a billiard ball.

"She doesn't want to play; she won't cooperate," whines the Tiger accusingly.

The Peacock is oblivious. Unimpressed with the whole scene, she lies there passed out on the backseat, a poor, scrawny, plebeian bird with wrecked plumage and sad breasts flattened by their own weight, her round, wigless skull exposed.

"These whores have deceived me," complains Nando Barragán childishly. "The Mermaid is a fraud and so is the blonde. This cruel world has left me only you, Tiger."

The Tiger revels in her victory and rises to the occasion by emitting low guttural sounds. She puts the Peacock's wig on Nando Barragán and she clings to his neck, licking him with her pink tongue like a kitten drinking warm milk from a saucer. She's still in the backseat and it's difficult for her to maintain a comfortable position; she leans forward over Nando, pressing her head against him, pinching his neck, breathing her foul breath on him; she knocks his glasses off his nose and tickles his ears with her long feline whiskers, impairing his driving ability.

The Tiger is not daunted by obstacles. She dedicates herself with renewed vigor to properly performing her function and manipulates his masculine features with obvious experience and guaranteed results. She plays arpeggios with her long fingers, flourishes with her soft fingertips, and massages him with her palms. Through the rearview mirror he watches her remove her tiger skin to reveal the human one beneath it, more wrinkled than the other but still possessing its own hidden attractions and secret delights, and he manages, finally, to achieve a satisfactory erection.

In perfect synchronization of man and machine, the Mercedes's velocity increases in tandem with its master's excitement, and with each careless turn of the steering wheel its nose peers over the abyss with suicidal abandon. After taking a curve that leaves the two left tires in midair, Nando slows down to check his speed and catch his breath, noting sadly that in doing so he has frustrated his already difficult ascent toward ejaculation.

"Sometimes it seems that you want to be down there," he says detachedly and lovingly to his automobile.

They have arrived at the highest point along the road. With the serenity of a grand gentleman accustomed to making drastic decisions without hesitation, Nando Barragán points the hood of his Mercedes toward the precipice, orders his passengers to disembark, and ejects himself with unexpected agility for a man of his size.

Colossal, powerful, and completely drunk, in the long blond wig like a Teutonic warrior, horrible and splendid, like the missing link, he pushes the vehicle toward the edge, looks at the shining sea below, swells his chest with air, and gives the final push.

The cream-colored Mercedes-Benz 500 SE falls into the abyss in a shower of sparks and crashes, offering a close-up, once-in-a-lifetime cinematographic spectacle, complete with special effects, while Nando watches in fascination as it flies gently through the limitless air. He watches it descend silently, in slow motion, striking sparks and decapitating angels along the way, bouncing softly off the black rocks, repeatedly demonstrating its Germanic solidity and unquestionable quality of craftsmanship, until at the end of its celestial journey the ocean waters receive it beneficently, cushioning the fall in their voluptuous bed, opening docilely to its triumphal passage in a happy effervescence of froth and bubbles, and swallow it whole, forever.

Above, from the edge of the precipice, Nando Barragán, the drunken yellow god, he of the magnificent blond wig and black sunglasses, with the Colt revolver in his belt, the craters in his skin, and the lame leg, contemplates the magnificent scene with his arms spread in the shape of a cross, a faraway look in his eyes, realizing that finally the moment of his ecstasy has arrived. He feels warm torrents of fluid inundating his body; he lets it flow in spurts, irrigating the planet with his seed. Then he lifts his tear-filled eyes toward the sky and, swelled with pride, shouts in a booming voice that is heard in heaven and hell:

"I'm an aaaaarrrtiiissst!"

"Is it true that there was still someone inside the car? They say that when he came back from the orgy in one of the Toyotas with his bodyguards, only Nando, the mariachis, the Mermaid, and the Tiger returned. The Peacock was never seen again."

"Since she was asleep, maybe she went over with the Mercedes and didn't wake up until she reached the bottom of the ocean. If she had been a mermaid, maybe she would have survived, but since she was only a yardbird . . ."

The musicians, who had been playing steadily the whole time in the Toyota, surround Nando, annoying him with *vallenatos*, following him wherever he goes like faithful shadows. Filled to the gills with Old Parr and exhausted after a cosmic orgasm produced by the voluntary destruction of a car worth a hundred thousand dollars, he decides to rest, like God on the seventh day of creation, and lies down to sleep in a soft patch of sand.

The musicians surround the sleeping man in adoration, softly singing boleros and other quiet songs, kneeling with their guitars and maracas, humble and solicitous, like Melchior, Gaspar, and Balthazar watching the Christ child sleep.

"Shut up, you sons of bitches! If you play one more note, I'll have you shot in a ditch!" shouts Nando, unable to sleep, cutting them off in the middle of a C-sharp. Soon after, he falls into a deep sleep, snoring like a wild beast and dreaming of Milena, the inaccessible.

"What happened to the Tiger and the Mermaid?"

"The bodyguards and musicians had their way with them while their boss slept."

◙ LOUIE GARCIA ROBINSON ◙

The Devil, Delfina Varela & the Used Chevy

Louie Garcia Robinson was born in El Paso, Texas, grew up in East Los Angeles, and currently lives in San Francisco. He has worked in public relations and as a newspaper reporter and magazine editor. This is from his debut novel, The Devil, Delfina Varela & the Used Chevy, *a true twentieth-century picaresque with a wide cast of Dickensian characters. Memo to Hollywood: It would make a great movie.*

RUY ASSESSED THE NEED TO TRIM MRS. BIRDWELL'S TALL HEDGES, which surrounded a swimming pool. The sides were O.K. but sometimes the tops—which could be seen from the second-story windows in the house—could be scraggly. He climbed a ladder to look at the tops of the hedges. He assessed them carefully. They could wait another week. What the heck. And then he peered below at something by the swimming pool. Ruy was dumbstruck. His eyes widened. What he saw was so phenomenal, so stunning, that he almost fell off of the ladder.

There before him was a wondrous sight: Mrs. Birdwell's spectacular daughter, Alexis, nude, sunning herself by the pool. Her body was covered with oil and her skin glistened. She lay on her back, covering her eyes with her right arm, her left leg crossing her right. And then she turned over slowly, carefully, revealing her backside before lying on her stomach. Ruy's vision intensified, tilted, and then began to sway. Here was Ruy's perfect, everlasting dream: a flawless young body triumphant and golden in the morning sun. Ruy could not breathe. He began to tremble. He descended carefully, sliding his wet palms along the sides of the ladder. When he was safely off the ladder he knelt on the wet earth and crossed himself with his right hand—from forehead to stomach, from left shoulder to right—bowed his head, folded his hands, and recited that lovely masterpiece: the prayer of St. Francis:

> *"Lord, make me an instrument of Your peace,*
> *Where there is hatred, let me sow love;*
> *Where there is injury, pardon . . ."*

It was as if Ruy had been allowed to witness a supernatural vision. He walked away. He could feel himself throbbing. He slipped into his truck, let it coast silently down the driveway before starting it and driving off. Alexis's unimaginable beauty was matched by an astonishing, perfect body. Ruy swallowed. His throat felt dry. He offered a silent prayer to all of the Holy Saints in Heaven, for he was grateful, sincerely grateful, for what he had just witnessed.

It was a difficult day for Ruy. The heat of the day matched the fervor of his thoughts. Every angle became Alexis's arms, Alexis's legs; every curve Alexis's proud, shimmering, tanned bottom. It was almost unfair. He felt so helpless, so trapped in his own cravings.

The slightest hint would force a vision of a honeyed body, arms, legs, a slow turning and then, only then, those two perfect golden roundnesses.

That night Ruy perspired. The night brought no relief. He couldn't sleep, it was simply too hot. There were too many concerns. Amapola had left him for that silly Pelon, who smoked those terrible cigars and cried like a baby. Lulusa, his dog, was being haughty to him. Molly the cat was picking up Lulusa's cues. She too was being nasty and distant. The property for one of the largest yards on his gardening route was being sold and he feared he would lose that income. And now his sister, Esmeralda, was calling him nightly with sad complaints about her new husband, Judge Abelardo Quintana.

"He doesn't love me. He doesn't want to do *anything*. He does not even want to make love to me anymore. We never go out. He hates to dance. He says it hurts his feet. Oh, Ruy, I thought I would be so happy. Instead I am so miserable. I am the most miserable person on this earth . . ."

But nothing distressed Ruy more than that day's apparition, that dream which taunted him, which followed him everywhere, which was just beneath the surface of everything he attempted. And it would play itself out in his mind once again, for the one thousandth time: Alexis's body, the angles of her arms and legs, to her backside and then her bottom: two perfect curves glistening defiantly in the morning sun. And then, just below that, almost as distant as a remembered echo or the wheezing of midnight surf, he could hear the words *"Mi hombre hermoso."*

Life could be so complicated, so terribly unfair. Not to mention the heat, the unrelenting heat.

It was all too much. Ruy dressed himself and got into his truck. When he turned on the truck's air-conditioning a puff of dust emerged from the vents along with grass clippings and bits of leaves. *Hijo*, he hadn't used the air conditioner in a long time. He drove aimlessly, distractedly. The cool air felt good on his face. That was better. And then he remembered his ladder. He had left his ladder next to the hedges overlooking Mrs. Birdwell's pool. He would retrieve it. That's what he would do, retrieve his ladder, perform something useful, something purposeful on this long and harrowing night.

He drove to the Birdwell house, which was totally dark. He would be careful, remove the ladder, and then slip away silently as he had done earlier.

When Ruy entered the backyard he could hear the burbling of the swimming pool's filtration system. It was so warm. A dip in the swimming pool would be nice. Yes. He would do it. In that total darkness he would slip silently into the water and cool off. He removed his clothes, wiped the perspiration from his face with his shirt and moved toward a corner of the pool where he reached out to touch the metal of a ladder railing. He turned, edged his way down the ladder, and entered the water carefully without making a sound until his entire naked body was floating like a contented, fat manatee. He moved slowly in the water without splashing. He was cool and comfortable for the very first time that day. He sighed.

And then there it was again, that persistent remembrance, the smell of vanilla, the maze of hair. Two arms embraced him in the water.

"*Mi hombre hermoso,*" whispered in perfect Spanish, and then an anxious mouth devouring his lips. The realization. The smell of vanilla. The slim waist, the hair. Ruy was dazed.

"Alexis!"

This can't be real, thought Ruy. It can't be possible. She was too beautiful, too refined, too young. He was too plain, too vulgar. This was only another false dream from which he would soon emerge. A trick. Reality would soon overpower this dream and serve up the usual main course of War, Famine, Pestilence, and Death; and side dishes of Racism, Poverty, and Bills. And for dessert: the Flu, Surly Waiters, Dental Hygiene, and, the worst calamity of all, Baldness.

But, no, this was real: the fragrance of vanilla, the long hair and she was there in the water with him, forming little circles in his ear with the tip of her tongue. Ruy could almost cry. Alexis had her arms and legs around him there in the water, by the shallow end of the pool. She was embracing him totally and she was nude.

"*Mi hombre hermoso,*" she kept repeating. And Ruy could feel the fine stirrings of a gallant, wondrous erection as a burble from the pool filtration system seemed to applaud and belch its approval.

And in a short while, they were out of the water and in her room and she was touching him, offering herself to him completely, whispering, "*Mi hombre hermoso,*" as she lowered herself over him, kissing him tenderly, guiding his erection into her own warmth. Ruy smiled. And then a powerful emotion swept over him. It was so overwhelming he almost cried as he offered a silent prayer. "Thank you, God. I thought for sure I was turning into a little *maricón.*"

And from some aromatic wilderness, Alexis was there stalking him, surrounding him with the fragrance of vanilla, creating small circles on his skin with her fingertips, touching him, caressing him and he was glad. Now she was over him and he was inside of her and her hair was touching his chest and there was a tightening and a low moan. And then he was very deep inside of her, wrapped in a vanilla cocoon and her words were there to tease him, to taunt him once again.

"*Mi hombre hermoso.*"

Never had the Spanish language sounded more beautiful. She had learned her flawless Castillian Spanish at the University of Salamanca. "*Mi hombre hermoso,*" she repeated, and it followed him even into his dreams of spectacular phantoms.

"*Te va gustar esto,*" said Alexis, and Ruy was pleased by the sound of her voice, her perfect Spanish.

On a starry night, Ruy could hear the mysterious sound of an owl *hoot-hoot-hooting*. Was this yet another dream from which he would soon be roused? Alexis was pressed against him and her body felt natural and right and his hand was touching something familiar and yet strange, a seed, a hard raisin between his fingertips, Alexis's nipple, as her mouth pressed against his. And yet another dream began to unfold. He heard the sigh of the owl. The superstitious Señora Talavera had once told him that a hooting owl was a sign of good fortune. And indeed it was. He never wanted this to end. As up somewhere, in Ruy's memory, the owl hooted approvingly. "I condone this, Ruy," said the owl. "A hoot to you for good luck and good fortune. She's a real knockout. *Hoot-hoot-hoot.*"

He was entangled in Alexis's long black hair, a web at his face; her soft hair was like a fine meshed net. Now her hair seemed to be windblown as it swept over his face. He didn't care. It was enough that it was brushing his face, sweeping over his warm eyelids, was touching his lips, his cheeks, his eyes and nose.

"A*iii*, Alexis," Ruy whispered.

It was all too good and, therefore, it would never last. And he knew it. He knew that at any moment it could all end, it would all be gone, disappear forever. The dream was too perfect. It would soon be a memory. Nothing more. There could be no other way. The bright star would burn out, explode into millions of pieces and rain down on him, and then everything would return to its previous darkness, tedium, melancholy, and isolation. The dance would be over, the play finished, the meal consumed. How could there ever be anything else? But for now, there was this, only this, and this alone. For now, this was all he ever wanted, even if it wouldn't last.

And then, from a dream of spice-filled barges floating slowly down a warm river past bright clusters of aromatic tropical flowers, there came a sensation of spinning, of circling, and he was falling, dropping straight down, only to loop out of his fall and then glide away pleasantly. Ruy emerged slowly from his dream. An expanding circle was being drawn on his stomach; a continuous series of spirals. Something was touching his fat, bare stomach and he awoke to see Alexis, her black hair nearly covering her green eyes.

She was smiling at him, rubbing her index finger around his belly button, and Ruy stretched like a sleek, contented cat. On that perfect morning, he felt boundless and strong as her leg rubbed against his thigh. At that very moment Ruy once again became all-powerful and invincible: immortal.

That day, in a supermarket, Ruy saw a ravishing woman. She was a striking beauty and she gave Ruy a perfect gift: a wonderful smile, and for the rest of the day Ruy was triumphant, for he had been touched by gods and goddesses and Alexis's firm breasts. Alexis's sex and aromas, still clinging to his lips, brought him great joy and another cascade of recollection.

What was to follow was the most lyrical period of Ruy's life, for is there anything sweeter than the process of making our own fresh discoveries of another person? It was a period of supreme Mexican elation. Ruy was thankful for everything he saw. Every sight was a joy. Each breath brought it all back: the sweetness of cinnamon and vanilla and, of course, nooky. His happiness was all-encompassing and he wanted to reach out and hug the world, the stars, and the moon. Everything moved gently and carefully in exquisite dance patterns of superb order and grace. Everything finally made such perfect sense.

"Poet" *from* The Cat and Other Stories

Beverly Silva was born in Los Angeles and is a longtime resident of San Jose. She is a poet, short story writer, teacher, and editor of anthologies. This is a piece called "Poet" from her story collection The Cat and Other Stories, *a volume that should be much better known by people much better than me. She is a good storyteller and much of her fiction has the bittersweet, tough-tender tone of a smart survivor.*

HE WAS A TERRIBLY NICE MAN. AS I SPENT THE EVENING OBSERVING him, I kept imagining that if I decided to crawl in bed with him he would take my hand gently and say, "My dear, it would afford me a great deal of pleasure if you would allow me the privilege of placing my penis in your vagina."

We met at a meeting of the Sexual Freedom League. My girlfriend, who is always trying to find me a respectable and financially well-off boyfriend, explained how cultured he was, and that I simply must attend their Wednesday night orientation meeting. She actually pressed the point so far that it became a matter of give it and/or him a try, or lose a friend.

The meeting was held in his home. He lived alone in a three bedroom house with a grand piano and a twenty-four foot swimming pool. Unfortunately, the leader of the group was ill, and many other members were away on vacation, so very little orientation was possible. Our host read a very long poem he had written about his ideal woman. Everyone liked it very much. His voice was a soft iambic with a slight European accent. The ladies felt the poem contained almost no male chauvinism, and everyone agreed that it expressed love and devotion without the destructive elements of jealousy and possessiveness. I waited patiently for the refreshments, and when the sesame seed cookies and herb tea were served, I began to count the hours of studying I had missed. I looked at my girlfriend and knew there was no way out. Her face was set. She had that "you are going to have a good time and meet nice people even if it kills you" look. I resigned myself to the fact that I could not afford to lose her friendship.

I even had to stay when the others left. Our host had been informed that I was doing graduate work in English literature and wanted my honest opinion of his writings. He re-read his poem to me along with others he found in a yellowed folder where he kept his musical compositions. I *was* impressed that he could read for so long in that soft iambic without a few deep breaths, but the nicest thing I could say about his poem was that a few trochees or spondees might add that certain touch. But I smiled at him instead and said, "They are very romantic." He beamed with pleasure.

He told me that his native home was Denmark, which made him much more culturally liberated than Americans, and thus he gave his utmost support to groups like the Sexual Freedom League.

He showed me the office where he did freelance engineering and the filing cabinet that contained his patents.

"It's very impressive," I said, which is what I always said when I felt I should be impressed when actually I was bored and understood nothing that was being explained to me. It usually satisfied people.

It did. He took me to the kitchen and removed a very modern uniquely designed fizz bottle from the refrigerator. It contained homemade champagne. He had sold the patent to Paul Masson. The dainty glasses he removed from a shelf held a thimble full of the drink. We sat back on the sofa in his living room where he placed the glasses on a table in front of us, which held a large vase of roses, a bunch of blue plastic grapes, and a bronze ashtray with the signs of the zodiac printed along the edge. He continued telling me about his lifestyle. His hobbies were writing poetry and music, and his socializing consisted of the more advanced singles groups, and occasional work at the Congregational Church.

"You live a very calm and orderly life," was all I could think of saying. My mind was on the untouched glasses in front of us, and I really wanted to say, do we drink this damn champagne or inhale it.

"You see," he continued, "God endowed me with this creativity, and I feel it is my duty to protect it. I do not smoke, I rarely drink, and I avoid extremes of any kind."

It's not always easy for me to keep my mouth shut and remember propriety. "Some of our greatest American writers were horrible drunks," I commented.

"Oh, Americans," he replied with the "Oh" coming close to a trochee sound.

I was forming a long list of European geniuses who were drunks, dopers, whorers, and everything else I could think of, when he asked me a question.

"Are you creative?"

I took the glass of champagne without an invitation and drank it as slowly as one can drink a thimble full of liquid while I dug deep for an answer. "Well, I do write some," I told him, "but my writings would probably be considered more as sociological documents than creative literature. They lack the romanticism of your poetry."

He moved closer to me. "It is so agreeable to meet an educated and appreciative woman," he stated.

Fuck propriety. "Do you think I could have a little more champagne?" I asked him.

"Of course," he said rising and taking my glass to the kitchen. "How thoughtless of me." He returned with another thimble full of the liquid. He placed it on the table. I picked it up, feeling like a very ill-bred woman, but also feeling somewhat more secure.

He once again moved closer to me. "In spite of my group involvements," he confided to me, "I'm really quite shy with women."

I finished drinking the champagne, and then carefully studied the glass.

He moved all the way towards me now, removed the glass from my hand, set it on the table, put his arm around my shoulder, and took my hand in his.

Before I could obey my impulse to retrieve my hand and rise, he looked me directly in the eyes for the first time, and had they always been that cold and blue? And he said to me, "Do you suck?"

I jumped up quickly, saying, "Excuse me for a moment," and

went to the kitchen. I reached into the first cupboard I saw, and luck was with me. I removed a very ordinary water glass. I opened the refrigerator and removed the fizz bottle. Pushing the button all the way down I soon had a large glass of champagne. Evidently my host was still on the sofa waiting for an answer. I leaned against the kitchen counter and drank the entire glass. I then returned to the living room.

He was on the sofa, much like a contented rabbit, showing no curiosity about my sudden departure. I looked him firmly in the eyes.

"Are you aware that your last words changed from iambic to a definite anapest?" I asked him.

He sat up startled, his eyes blinking at me, and his nose definitely twitching.

There appeared to be no way out of this now except through the English teacher route, sophomorish as it was. "American writers," I told him, "often use very extreme language. In my own writings, for example, I make use of a strong spondee. Fuck you!"

I then excused myself by claiming a mild case of gastritis brought on by the champagne and I left. I drove to the nearest bar where I met a man who assured me he had never tasted sesame seed cookies. He bought me five brandy alexanders while I told him the whole sordid tale of my favorite uncle who was found knifed by his third wife's lover. We went to his apartment later. He wasn't very cultured, but he was a terribly nice man.

❧ SHEILA ORTIZ TAYLOR ❧

Coachella

Sheila Ortiz Taylor was born in Los Angeles in 1939. In addition to a B.A., M.A., and Ph.D., she holds a degree in judo and says she wore six guns as a child. Her novel, Coachella, *seems at times so quiet, so graceful, so full of ease that you don't realize just how good (and complex) it is.*

MARINA SEES THE LIGHT GLOWING IN HER OWN KITCHEN, BUT Yolanda's place looks dark. And yet her car is parked in its usual place, out under the palo verde. Yo has a ship's bell by the door decorated with strings of dried chiles and Indian corn. Plants in pots everywhere. Little lemon tree. Marina sounds the clapper against the bell once, leans on the side of the trailer breathing hard. Carolina startles. In a moment the door opens. The kitchen light flicks on.

"¿Estás durmiendo?" Marina asks. Yo's hair is awhirl with cowlicks.

"No, working. Thinking. Come on in. What time is it anyway? You okay? How's Carolina?"

"We're fine. We were out. . . . It's just that. . . . " Marina stands with the baby, hesitant. Maybe she should leave. She glimpses sheets of graph paper all over the kitchen table, an open blue notebook, a green pen with the cap off. Old-fashioned; a fountain pen.

179

"¿Has comido?" Yo asks.

"Sí, sí, pero you go ahead. I think we better . . ."

They are standing in the dark. Yo leans toward her and kisses her tenderly on the mouth. Marina had not expected this and yet she has been waiting for this. There is a softness and a warmth that she could not have foreseen, that keep her rooted to the spot, un-comprehending.

Yo lifts Carolina out of the backpack, snugs her in close, sways with her. "She's out like a light. Shall I put her down? Can you stay a minute?"

Marina follows Yo down the hall to her bedroom, rousing herself enough to take mental pictures in the dim light so that later she can take them out and study them. The double bed covered by an Indian blanket, the Japanese lantern hanging over the two pillows, the cane-bottom chair with a pair of Levi's tossed over the back.

Yo puts Carolina down on her bed, places the chair against the outside edge. Marina shrugs out of the child carrier, leaves it on the bed. The room smells of incense and of Yo.

As Marina starts down the hall following Yo, suddenly Yo stops and Marina glides into her, feels herself led, gently, somehow into the small office where—within a dome of shadows and books— she feels Yo's arms around her and herself opening like a cactus flower, feels a hot current running inside her. They are kissing and her mouth is opening, and she is all over hot petals and sizzling liquids: agua caliente.

Rain of Scorpions and Other Stories

Estela Portillo Trambley's "Rain of Scorpions" is a classic of Chicano literature. And, as befits the work, which so movingly and eloquently is about tradition, it is a tale full of the old-fashioned— in the best sense—virtues: strength, honesty, intelligence, and passion. (OK, go ahead and call me a sentimentalist, I don't care.)

LUPE HAD FIXED A CHICKEN CASSEROLE FOR SUPPER, AND MAMÁ Chita had taken some next door for Fito's supper, then gone off to rosary services. Lupe no longer went with her. More and more, God was becoming an abstraction, a belief of the mind, so Lupe's faith was no longer intact. Perhaps she had read too much. But Mamá Chita's radiance was faith. God touched her shoulder each day and that gave la abuelita her sense of well-being.

After the supper dishes were done, Lupe showered and shampooed her hair. She wrapped her hair in a towel and put on a light wrap to sit in the flower room. She must not miss the sunset. She took her guitar just in case the sunset was too beautiful. At times like that she had to free the world with music. The sun was going down. It dusted the walls of houses pink and made the elm seem as if it were on fire.

Lupe looked out into the coming night. Her eyes fell on a dog sniffing the residue of scorpions lumped up against the edge of the sidewalk. Old Estevan, hauling a dismembered chair, stopped long enough to wish her a good evening. The sun was down and the brilliant hues of the sky filled the horizon. At a distance, tattered gray clouds hung between trees.

The moon rose full and orange as dusk overwhelmed the colors of the sky. Shadows danced between light and dark in the already moon-soaked porch. The breathing of her plants anointed the air. She closed her eyes, breathing deeply. The smell of tar mixed with the scents of honeysuckle and gardenias. Raising her arms, silver in the moonlight, she stretched. It was her favorite time.

Across in Fito's house, the bedroom light was on. Sitting down on an old cane chair, she untoweled her hair. After rubbing the long silky strands vigorously with the cloth, she sat back and closed her eyes again.

After a while she looked up thoughtfully to contemplate the pink horizon sinking on the turn of the earth. Yes, she must play. She began strumming ever so softly. A song rose to her throat, an old Indian melody, "All in a circle within me, the newborn child, the fallen tree . . ." Then she stopped to weave and stitch pieces of memory.

Lupe, the child among children, following her Pied Piper, Fito, to Papá At's where he bought nieve raspada for all of them. The taste of the sweet melting against her tongue, Fito's eyes, amber, illumed by the sun, Fito's confident laugh and his gentleness with children; pieces, little pieces, making the claim of love; and she, speechless as all children are when feeling shy, grieved in a silence even then.

There was the girl, Lupe, walking home from school, lingering against the red elm, Fito's arm brushing her cheek, his palm against the tree, his eyes, alive, liquid with a tenderness, confiding to her . . . so close, so close. She could not breathe for love, but she could not tell him how he kindled her with his presence for what he confided was like a knife gashing her heart. He told her of his love for Belén, his consuming passion for the lovely Belén, the only existing universe for him. Always Belén, Belén, Belén. Lupe, silent, would wonder, How many times have I measured life in tears?

She had sat at parties with cold, listless hands in her lap, forgotten. Not being asked to dance—the little girl in her cried and wanted to vanish from the earth. And when she saw Fito holding Belén's slender body in his arms, Lupe would shrivel and fade until she could bear it no more; then she would run out into the night. The music mocked; the moonlight mocked; the blending of honeysuckle and love song filtering out into the street hurt, hurt so much. She would sob her loneliness, and when there were no more tears, there was comfort from the stillness. Only the tapping of her heels would echo sharply on cold cement as she walked home alone.

Lupe shook herself free of sad memories. She began to brush her hair, a dark silk cloud around her face. Then she picked up the guitar again. Music was a kind of solace. She really believed that music was a proof of some kind of heaven.

Belén was gone. Fito felt he was not whole because of his leg. Lupe wanted to make him feel whole. He was whole and beautiful, but there was no more Belén. Love me, Fito, she commanded fiercely in her mind. I know about the love that counts because I have passed through the fire of loneliness. That has made me whole. Now, let me make you whole . . .

In dreams, Fito was hers. How many times had he surfaced in her sleep? His touch, his smile were for her then. Strange, how her desire would flow. In her sleep, there was a symphony of minds, bodies, free, in a world before the world. She saw him, smelled him, touched him, heard him, a love dance, a starkness burning. Don't wake—dream on and on and on, night out of time. Don't wake. But she would awaken, grasping in the darkness for something gone, her mind tracing reasons, ways to dream again. At times night would become the living part of her, passions breathing the full-blown fragrance of his presence, sinews, skin, heartbeat.

This night her thoughts had run into the music. She looked up at the light in Fito's room. All things were in accord, the circle within, the circle without. Love? What did she know of love? The alphabet of love was undecipherable to her. Yet, the night was interlaced with dreams. She conjured them up again and again to give substance to her day. He had kissed her the night of the meeting. He no longer kept the picture of Belén on the nightstand by his bed.

Barefooted, hair loosened, holding the thin wrap around her body, she made her way to his door.

In Praise of the Stepmother

Mario Vargas Llosa is Peru's foremost author. The publication of his first novel, The Time of the Hero, *in 1962, established him as an important voice, and* The Green House *(awarded the Gallegos Award—South America's most important literary prize—in 1967) gave him worldwide acclaim. This is from* In Praise of the Stepmother, *his recent erotic fable.*

SOAPING HERSELF, SHE FONDLED HER BIG STRONG BREASTS, THE erect nipples, and her still-graceful waist, from which the ample curves of her hips opened out, like two halves of a fruit, and her thighs, her buttocks, her armpits with the hair removed, and her long smooth neck with one solitary mole. "I shall never grow old," she prayed, as she did each morning at her bath. "Even if it means having to sell my soul or anything else. I shall never be ugly or miserable. I shall die beautiful and happy." Don Rigoberto had convinced her that saying, repeating, and believing these things would make them come true. "Sympathetic magic, my love." Lucrecia smiled: her husband might be a little eccentric, but, in all truth, a woman never tired of a man like that.

All the rest of the day, as she gave orders to the servants, went shopping, visited a woman friend, lunched, made and received phone calls, she wondered what to do with the child. If she gave his secret away to Rigoberto, he would turn into her enemy and then the old premonition of a domestic hell would become a reality. Perhaps the most sensible thing to do was to forget Justiniana's revelation and, adopting a cool aloofness, gradually undermine the fantasies the boy had woven around her, no doubt only half aware that that was what they were. Yes, that was the prudent thing to do: say nothing, and, little by little, distance herself from him.

That afternoon, when Alfonsito, back from school, came to kiss her, she quickly turned her cheek away and buried herself in the magazine she was leafing through, without asking him how his classes had gone or if he had homework for the next day. Out of the corner of her eye, she saw his little face pucker up in a tearful pout. But she was not moved and that night she let him eat his dinner alone, without coming downstairs to keep him company as she often did (she rarely ate dinner herself). Rigoberto phoned her a little later, from Trujillo. All his business deals had gone well and he missed her lots. He would miss her even more that night, in his dreary room in the Hotel de Turistas. Nothing new there at home? No, nothing. Take good care of yourself, darling. Doña Lucrecia listened to a bit of music, alone in her room, and when the child came to bid her good night, she coldly bade him the same. Shortly thereafter, she told Justiniana to prepare the bubble bath she always took before going to bed.

As the girl drew the bathwater and she undressed, the feeling of apprehension that had dogged her footsteps all day came to the fore again, much stronger now. Had she done the right thing by treating

Fonchito as she had? Despite herself, it pained her to remember the look of hurt and surprise on his little face. But wasn't that the only way to put a stop to childish behavior that threatened to become dangerous?

She was half asleep in the tub, immersed up up her neck, stirring the swirls of soap bubbles with a hand or a foot, when Justiniana knocked on the door: might she come in, señora? Doña Lucrecia watched her approach, a towel in one hand and a dressing gown in the other, with a frightened look on her face. She realized immediately what the girl was about to whisper to her: Fonchito is up there, señora. She nodded and with an imperious wave of her hand ordered Justiniana out of the room.

She lay in the water without moving for a long time, carefully 7not looking up. Ought she to look? Should she point her finger at him? Cry out, call him names? She could hear the clatter behind the dark glass cupola overhead; see in her mind's eye the little kneeling figure, his fright, his feeling of shame. She could hear his strident scream, see him break into a run. He would slip, fall into the garden with the roar of a rocket exploding. The sudden thud of his little body as it hit the balustrade, flattened the croton hedge, caught in the witchy-fingered branches of the datura would reach her ears. "Make an effort, control yourself," she said to herself, clenching her teeth. "Don't create a scandal. Keep clear, above all, of something that might end in tragedy."

She was trembling with anger from head to foot and her teeth were chattering, as though she were chilled to the bone. Suddenly she rose to her feet. Not covering herself with the towel, not cowering so that those invisible little eyes would have no more than an imperfect, fleeting vision of her body. No, quite the contrary;

187

she stood up on tiptoe, parting her legs, and before emerging from her bath she stretched, revealing herself generously, obscenely, as she removed her plastic bath cap and loosed her long hair with a toss of her head. And on stepping out of the bathtub, instead of donning her dressing gown immediately, she stood there naked, her body gleaming with tiny drops of water, tense, daring, furious. She dried herself very slowly, limb by limb, rubbing the towel over her skin again and again, leaning to one side, bending over, halting at times as though distracted by a sudden idea, in a posture of indecent abandon, or contemplating herself carefully in the mirror. And with the same lingering, maniacal care she then rubbed her body with moisturizing lotions. And as she thus displayed herself before the invisible observer, her heart pulsed with wrath. What are you doing, Lucrecia? What is the meaning of these affected poses, Lucrecia? But she went on exposing herself, as she had never done before to anyone, not even to Don Rigoberto, moving from one side of the bathroom to the other at a slow, deliberate pace, naked, as she brushed her hair and her teeth and sprayed herself with cologne. As she played the leading role in this improvised spectacle, she had the presentiment that what she was doing was also a subtle way of punishing the precocious libertine crouched in the darkness up above, with images of an intimacy that would shatter, once and for all, that innocence that served him as an excuse for his boldness.

When she climbed into bed, she was still trembling. She lay there for a long time, unable to sleep, missing Rigoberto. She felt thoroughly displeased with what she had done; she positively detested the boy and forced herself not to divine the meaning of those hot flashes that, from time to time, electrified her nipples. What's happened to you, woman? She did not recognize herself. Could it be because she'd turned forty? Or a consequence of those nocturnal fantasies and bizarre caprices of her husband's? But it was all Alfonsito's fault. That child is corrupting me, she thought, disconcerted.

When, finally, she managed to drop off to sleep, she had a voluptuous dream that seemed to bring to life one of those etchings in Don Rigoberto's secret collection that he and she were in the habit of contemplating and commenting upon together at night, seeking inspiration for their love.

Hot Soles in Harlem

Emilio Díaz Valcárcel was born in Puerto Rico in 1929. He has won awards for his writing in both America and Spain as well as his native land. Hot Soles in Harlem *is one of the best books, dealing with a Puerto Rican immigrant who comes to New York City and immediately gets involved in adventures and misadventures.*

SEEING HER SEATED SIMPLY HE SENSED THE PERFUME OF THE RICE powder, her simple cologne, her gleaming skin, without makeup, seemed to smile at him and, in fact, she looked at him smilingly joyous defenseless frank soft delicate when, without saying a word, he took her hands and made her stand up. In reality, Gerardo did the following:

1. He took her by the hands (to do so had to lean over slightly, because he is almost six feet tall).

2. He made her stand up gently.

3. Without smiling, without haste, he reached out his left hand and unbuttoned the top button of her brown coat (a frankly loathsome color).

4. When he opened the third button from the top, he pushed it aside to uncover her chest. He found that she had fulfilled the

191

agreement sealed with a kiss in the storeroom: she was wearing absolutely nothing between her coat and her skin. So he saw her bounteous (this is how they are usually described by poets who respect themselves) protruding breasts, full, the small hairs raised in expectant pleasure, the nipples hardened. Gerardo controlled himself to keep his cool, you know, do it right to the end, keep from leaning over immediately and touching the space between her breasts with his tongue, circle each resplendent nipple with the red flag of his tongue . . .

5. With a slightly trembling left hand, almost stiffly, he unbuttoned the three remaining buttons from top to bottom.

6. He proceeded to pull open her coat so that her solid brown body with disturbing roundnesses appeared before his blue eyes.

7. Without breathing, he pulled himself out of his shoes without tremblingly jumping out of them, pushing one against the other, without even leaning over, and extricated himself this time with a little more haste from his shirt and then unbuckled his belt and let his nice corduroy pants slide to the floor along with the boxer shorts wide like panties, he lifted his legs one by one — if he did it at once, he'd kill himself! The old Botticelli couldn't have imagined such a birth of Venus: Caty on a lovely shell, a so humbly tropical Lorenzo di Medici seeing her to the depths, in reality gazing at the ineffable foxy Vespucci and then their two bodies came close until they grazed touching each other on their hot spots a sea of sensitivity: her breasts against his smooth hard breast, his penis — what do you expect! — perfectly erect touching her perfumed hair-covered fleshy triangle, then they come even closer and touch face to face in the center of the room, without having turned on the light of course but with enough light coming in from the street,

two well-defined bodies in the middle of a late Harlem afternoon, solid, sturdy, burning itself in an advanced September of streets stiff with the most noisy and spoken and wordy silence ever experienced by any Boricua lover whatsoever, the words caught fire in their noble youthful minds and acquired a blinding density illuminated hidden interstices and then burned out as they fell like shooting stars while words continuously arose which repeated the preceding process and mixed with one another, they imposed themselves and competed in brilliance, it seemed that each one sustained a fiery contest of wits shadowy without sonorous words formed by luminous features

filaments of sunshine
a starry substance
the central nerve of a column of fire
wordfire in the perfumed Boricuan night
a luminous thread escaped from a furious bolt of lightning atop
    the peak of El Yunque
the heat arising from the raging heart of we'll say a
    Guatemalan volcano

Chichicastenango: the first two syllables of this indigenous name suggests unions similar to Gerardo and Caty's: they join further, their mouths seek each other, touch, connect, and Gerardo's tongue makes an excursion beneath her teeth, he makes it move with precision over her lower teeth rubbing her moist lip from one side to the other, he does the same with her upper lip, which he pulls a little, takes it between his, and then runs it over the area behind her teeth, including the palate, with his excellent boneless instrument—the tongue—at the same time Caty retreats slowly, united in a progressive dance that carries them inevitably, fatally, not to the door, naturally, but to the white bed, which jumps for joy beside the half-lit window, and to the sheet that receives the girl's buttocks first, then her back, then her slightly bashful and separated legs in some miraculous way without there being a crash of both bodies because Gerardo, inconceivably conquering the force of gravity, remained attached the whole time to the descending body so that they both landed united on the bed in an almost floating violent manner, without striking it, but rather proceeding downward from the inevitable biped verticality in a progressively inclining manner until they achieved the horizontality dreamed of by souls moved by desire, and then he begged her to personally take his organ and place it where it belonged, and he felt Caty's fingers take it with a dexterity not excluding caution and place it there, in the burning moist cavity and then she gently moved her hips upward in such a manner that he responded with a swordlike thrust, penetrating her with a certain violence which made her retreat instinctively and moan, but Gerardo persisted with his assault until they reached a fundamental agreement: he would move downward and in a circular motion and she would move upward and in an inverse circular direction, so that the music of the dance did not wait for the music from upstairs, the music of the almost shouted rock with guitars that whined and drums that beat, and then the tempo picked up and the drums beat dryly making the room vibrate

the guitar humanly absorbed all of the accelerated rhythm
without a definable melody

the rhythm was unsustainable the drums desperately sounded
    fired a long drum roll
The guitar vibrated to its most recondite string
wrapped in this inexpressible violent rhythm he she rhythm rock
    an ancient muscular knot released
a discharge of flowing burning electricity shakes the room loud
    low music escapes
he exhausted she exhausted they smile one on top of the other
    sweaty satisfied
because there's nothing like music to sedate the nerves and make
    people love happily into delirium

Naked Ladies

Alma Luz Villanueva has been called "the quintessential feminist author, continuously dedicated to the search for a universal female community." She is also one of the most prolific and most honored of Chicana writers and has won many literary awards. She lives in Santa Cruz, California. This is from Naked Ladies.

ALTA TURNED, FACING HIM, TOOK HIS FACE IN HER HANDS, AND slowly kissed his eyelids, both his cheeks, and then, seeing the startled look in Doug's eyes, she kissed him softly on his silent lips.

Doug groaned loudly and reached his arms around Alta, feeling her strong, slender back with his hands, clutching her to him, feeling her living woman's warmth. He felt like crying for joy: her touch, her touch. He felt like worshipping her. He felt she might disappear. No, no, not that, he pleaded silently. He buried his face in her neck. And then he smelled her woman's smell, her juices gathering, hidden, but he could smell it.

He was afraid, but he had to do it; he would die if she wouldn't let him enter her body. If she wouldn't shelter him, he would die. He put a hand over her breast, caressing her softly, and she quivered, throwing her head back with a cry of pleasure. He began to kiss her neck gently, then with wide open sucking motions, tasting

197

her. He licked her neck, lifted her sweater, and he saw she wore no bra and her breasts were brown and beautiful, almost girlish. He sucked them, being careful not to lose control because he felt he would devour her if he did.

Alta shut the front room door with her free hand and then, extending herself fully, lay back on the couch inviting him. They kissed again and again. Neither spoke. This was the Braille of compassion and sympathy. Human comfort.

Doug tugged at her jeans, unbuttoning the top and lowering the zipper. He exposed her belly and plunged his tongue into her belly button, and she began to move under him. Her smell was stronger now. He was closer. He slipped the jeans down past her hips and carefully lowered the silky, red panties. Seeing her woman's hair, he moaned, spreading her thighs with his large hands. Then he opened the plum colored labia and saw the fleshy queen waiting to be kissed, to be stroked, to be sucked and licked. To be worshipped.

And he was more than willing. His excitement mounted as hers mounted, and the more he ate her, the more he wanted her, so when she came, shuddering violently and crying out, his penis, his prick, was in pain.

He lifted himself to enter her blindly, but Alta stopped him. "Wait, take your clothes off and lie on the rug. Please," she asked, looking into his eyes.

Alta stripped everything off and when she turned to face Doug, he was lying on the rug with one leg up trying to shield his erect penis as though he were suddenly embarrassed by its swollen presence. She knelt down, taking it into both her hands, feeling its heat, shaft to tip. A small bit of sperm was gathered at its tip and she licked it, trailing her tongue down the rough underside. She marveled at its stiffness, putting it between her soft breasts, and then she sucked it gently.

"Let me come inside you, Alta. I can't stand it," Doug pleaded, sitting up, braced by his elbows. His face was diffuse and lovely. His penis was long and lovely. Lovely. Full of sperm. Full of life. His life.

"Take the rubber band out of your hair." Doug's thick, golden hair spread luxuriously over his neck. It was exactly as Alta had thought; he was beautiful. Quickly, she mounted him, putting his penis at the opening of her cunt and teasing him by holding it there. Her opening was hot and inviting; she wanted him. She smiled at him. "Do you want to come in?"

Doug's head was thrown back, his thick hair spread on the rug. He gripped her ass, and his arms and chest revealed their strength. He locked eyes with her, almost angrily. "What do you think?" he answered huskily.

Alta lowered herself, as Doug moaned and cried out, sobbing wildly, until he filled her completely with his life. And then they fucked. Ripples and ripples of unending pleasure flowed between them as she raised and lowered herself, watching his cock disappear; and he, for a moment, becoming a woman like herself; and she, with his hardness, for a moment, becoming a man; and then she utterly feminine, being penetrated; and then he utterly masculine, penetrating; and then peace. And then they fucked again. This was the comfort of the living. Woman to man. Cock to cunt.

❧ Acknowledgments ❧

Excerpt from *The Killing of the Saints* by Alex Abella. Copyright © 1991 by Alex Abella. Used by permission of Crown Publishers, a division of Random House, Inc.

Excerpt from *The Infinite Plan* by Isabel Allende. Copyright © 1991 by Isabel Allende. English language translation copyright © 1993 by HarperCollins Publishers, Inc. Reprinted by permission of HarperCollins Publishers, Inc. For additional territory/ rights contact Agencia Literaria Carmen Balcells, S.A., Diagonal 580, Barcelona 08021.

Excerpt from *In the Name of Salomé*. Copyright © 2000 by Julia Alvarez. Published by Algonquin Books of Chapel Hill. Reprinted by permission of Susan Bergholz Literary Services, New York. All rights reserved.

Excerpt from *Dona Flor and Her Two Husbands* by Jorge Amado, translated by Federico do Onis. Copyright © 1969 by Alfred A. Knopf, Inc. Used by permission of Alfred A. Knopf, a division of Random House, Inc.

Excerpt from *Zia Summer* by Rudolfo Anaya. Copyright © 1995 by Rudolfo Anaya. Reprinted by permission of Warner Books, Inc.

Excerpt from "The Areopagite's Story" from *The Color of Summer* by Reinaldo Arenas, translated by Andrew Hurley. Copyright © 2000 by Andrew Hurley and the Estate of Reinaldo Arenas. Original, *El Color del Verano* © 1990 by Reinaldo Arenas. Used by permission of Viking Penguin, a division of Penguin Putnam Inc.

Excerpt from *Peel My Love Like an Onion*. Copyright © 1999 by Ana Castillo. Published by Doubleday, a division of Random House, Inc. Reprinted by permission of Susan Bergholz Literary Services, New York. All rights reserved.

Excerpt from *To Die in Berlin* by Carlos Cerda. Copyright © 1999 Carlos Cerda. Translated by Andrea G. Labinger. Reprinted by permission of Latin American Literary Review Press, Pittsburgh.

Excerpt from *Chicano Chicanery* by Daniel Chacón. Copyright © 2000 by Daniel Chacón. Used by permission of Arte Público Press—University of Houston, Houston.

Excerpt from *Face of an Angel*. Copyright © 1994 by Denise Chávez. Published by Warner Books and originally in hardcover by Farrar, Straus & Giroux. Reprinted by permission of Susan Bergholz Literary Services, New York. All rights reserved.

Excerpt from *Drown* by Junot Díaz. Copyright © 1996 by Junot Díaz. Used by permission of Revered Books, a division of Penguin Putnam Inc.

Excerpt from *Like Water for Chocolate* by Laura Esquivel. Copyright © 1992 by Doubleday, a division of Bantam, Doubleday, Dell Publishing Group, Inc. Used by permission of Doubleday, a division of Random House, Inc.

Excerpt from "Venecia's Passage to Heaven" from *Eccentric Neighborhoods* by Rosario

Acknowledgments

Ferré. Copyright © by Rosario Ferré. Reprinted by permission of Farrar, Straus and Giroux, LLC.

Excerpt from *Your Name Written on Water* by Irene González Frei, translated by Kristina Cordero. Copyright © 1999 by Kristina Cordero. Used by permission of Grove/Atlantic, Inc.

Excerpt from "Parque de la Llama: 1938" from *The Years with Laura Díaz* by Carlos Fuentes, translated by Alfred Mac Adam. Translation copyright © 2000 by Farrar, Straus and Giroux, LLC. Reprinted by permission of Farrar, Straus and Giroux, LLC.

Excerpt from *The Agüero Sisters* by Cristina García. Copyright © 1997 by Cristina García. Used by permission of Alfred A. Knopf, a division of Random House, Inc.

Excerpt from *Sultry Moon* by Mempo Giardinelli. Copyright © by Mempo Giardinelli. Reprinted by permission of Guillermo Schavelzon Agencia Literaria & Associados.

Excerpt from *The Long Night of White Chickens* by Francisco Goldman. Copyright © 1992 by Francisco Goldman. Used by permission of Grove/Atlantic, Inc.

Excerpt from *The Street of Night* by Lucia Guerra. Copyright © 1997 by Lucia Guerra. Reprinted by permission of Garnet Publishing, Reading U.K.

Excerpt from "Nothing to Do" from *Dirty Havana Trilogy* by Pedro Juan Gutiérrez, translated by Natasha Wimmer. Translation copyright © 2001 by Natasha Wimmer. Reprinted by permission of Farrar, Straus and Giroux, LLC.

Excerpt from "In the Hotel Splendor 1980" from *The Mambo Kings Play Songs of Love* by Oscar Hijuelos. Copyright © 1989 by Oscar Hijuelos. Reprinted by permission of Farrar, Straus and Giroux, LLC.

Excerpt from *Two Crimes* by Jorge Ibargüengoitia, translation by Asa Zatz. Copyright © Asa Zatz. Originally published by David R. Godine Publisher Inc. Reprinted by permission of Asa Zatz. All rights reserved.

Excerpt from *Paradiso* by José Lezama Lima, translated by Gregory Rabassa. Translation copyright © 1974 by Farrar, Straus and Giroux, Inc. Reprinted by permission of Farrar, Straus and Giroux, LLC.

Excerpt from *Cantora* by Sylvia López-Medina. Copyright © 1992 by Sylvia López-Medina. Reprinted by permission of The University of New Mexico Press.

Excerpt from *Twilight at the Equator* by Jamie Manrique. Copyright © 1999 by Jamie Manrique. Reprinted by permission of The Malaga Baldi Literary Agency.

Excerpt from *Love in the Time of Cholera* by Gabriel García Márquez, translated by Edith Grossman. Copyright © 1988 by Alfred A. Knopf, Inc. Used by permission of Alfred A. Knopf, Inc.

Excerpt from *Las Tumbas (The Tombs)* by Enrique Medina. Copyright © 1993 by Enrique Medina. Translated by David William Foster. Reproduced by permission of Routledge, Inc., part of The Taylor & Francis Group.

Excerpt from "The Tramp Steamer's Last Port of Call" in *The Adventures of Maqroll: Four Novellas**** by Alvaro Mutis and translated by Edith Grossman. Copyright © 1995 by Alvaro Mutis. Translation copyright © by Edith Grossman. Reprinted by permission of HarperCollins Publishers, Inc. *Amirbar; The Tramp Steamer's Last Port of Call; Abdul Bashur, Dreamer of Ships; Triptych on Sea and Land. For